The Eight slopes of Chanukah

Jacqueline Elisabeth

To the ski squad. This book wouldn't be what it is without you.

Chapter One

"Are you sure you're not forgetting anything?" my mom asked as she appeared in my doorway. She was always like this. We have been going on this trip for over ten years, yet every single year she acts as if I don't know how to pack for myself. Every year she hands me the most organized packing list that has everything on it that I could possibly need for a week trip. She'll even ignore the fact that we normally do laundry on the trip and make sure I overpack.

I sighed and turned to look at her. She looked tired. We all did. "I'm almost eighteen, Mom, I know how to pack for myself," I replied with a sigh. This had almost become a ritual we would do every year. No matter what, I know she's going to unpack and repack my suitcase to double- and triple-check that I have packed everything I need and everything she can think of that I might need in an emergency.

"And no bringing your laptop this year," she said with a smile, eliciting a grunt from me in response. "We are going to have some quality family time on this vacation." Though we both knew that wouldn't actually last. She'll forget before we even get to Utah.

"So how many books is too many books?" I retorted. I know she doesn't like how much I read when we're all together as a family. Don't get me wrong, she loves that I love to read. She is more than willing to pay for all the books I could want, but quality family time means no electronics, no books, and saying goodbye to our friends after dinner and playing a card game or video game or even watching a movie or TV show. The exact details of what we end up doing when we're together as a family may vary, but at least we'll be together.

She sighed and gave me a look I knew all too well—a look that said, 'when did my baby girl become such a grown woman.' "Enough," she said briefly with a smile.

When my sister, Evangeline, died, books became my biggest form of escapism. It became easy for me to lose myself in a book and sit in a different world for hours. Though I love the occasional fantasy novel, getting a chance to dive into another world is always something that can take me out of the world I'm currently in. I have found that I love nothing more than contemporary and romance novels. There is something so magical about everyday life that is encapsulated in those books and makes me feel as though I'm not alone.

When I started this reading frenzy just days after Evangeline's passing, I started with the books she had in her room. The ones she had read, the ones she had loved, and the ones she had yet to read. Those were the ones I gravitated to the most. There was something in all those books. Her intent to read them was evident by the way they had been placed on her nightstand. It was almost as if I could feel her excitement to read them by just simply picking up the book and holding it in my hands.

When we were little, we had different reading tastes. She always went straight for the fantasy, and as I've mentioned, I do read fantasy, but it's not a genre I really love, so I gravitated toward romance and mystery novels. We used to sit together when we were on vacation, poring over the books, reading one after the other. And in Park City, we would make it a must to go to Dolly's Bookstore, one of my favorite spots. And yet this year, the thought of going there just isn't as exciting. The thought of going there feels empty and lonely, and like I'm leaving behind one of the most important things in my world; my sister. It almost feels wrong to go without her. It feels wrong for me to go spend hours scouring the shelves looking for my next read, knowing she isn't right beside me doing the same thing. It will feel weird without her recommendations and the way she used to try and convince me that I should read more fantasy. "You just haven't found the right fantasy novel yet." She would always say and then place three into my hands. Whatever she recommended, I read, no matter how much I hated it.

For the longest time, I thought reading fantasy novels might make me feel closer to her, especially after her death, but if anything, they made me feel the same as they had back when she used to try and convince me to read some of her favorites. They just made me feel farther from her and reminded me of how we would never be able to relate to each other when it came to books. She would never like my favorite novels, and I would never like hers.

She never liked stories that were real. She always wanted to be transported to another world. It was how she dealt with all the bullying she had to face in elementary and middle school. She could read a book that took place in a world that was so far away that she herself could be there only for a few minutes. She would be able to be transported to a place where she knew she would be loved and accepted no matter what.

I never felt that way about books. I always found those other worlds to be confusing. They never made sense to me, and they always took me out of the story with the way I had to try extra hard to be able to put everything together in my head. I needed books to be straightforward. I needed the world to be one I already knew, or it would get so confusing I would lose my mind. But I tried so hard. I wanted to read those books more than anything. I wanted to feel close to her. I wanted to know how she felt when she was reading those books, and I wanted to feel the same way.

But now, books don't remind me of what I've lost. I know eventually I will find her again through a book, even if I am the one who has to write it. Now, I always turn to fantasy novels. Every time I flip the page in whatever book I'm reading, I can feel her glancing over my shoulder, reading along with me.

No one warned me what to expect when my sister died. No one told me that I should have been prepared for the physical pain that comes with grief. No one prepared me for the overwhelming way I'm always fighting to breathe. The way that if my thoughts wander, just for a second, I'll realize I can't remember the sound of her laugh anymore. And it's only been six months. It used to be so easy to conjure up in my head, but now I have to think about it. No one prepared me for the way each little thing forgotten feels like losing her all over again. How each little thing means I'm farther and farther from my built-in best friend. From the one person above all else I was supposed to protect.

And now I'm sitting here, packing for this trip that was always her favorite. During her favorite holiday. With the gifts that I spent the past year planning for her and our friends. A holiday that wasn't ever a big deal became such a deal for us because of the traditions and love we added to this time of year. Most of that was Evangeline. It's weird not having her next to me, packing alongside me, reminding me of everything I'm forgetting. Well, everything she's realized she's forgotten and needs to make sure I didn't also forget.

It's hard to not feel as though she's slipping through my fingers.

We have been going on an annual ski trip since Evangeline was five years old. My mother always believed that skiing was important. She grew up near the mountains and spent all of her weekends in the winters skiing with her friends. She always wanted that for us, I guess. It was something that was important to her, so why wouldn't she have wanted it for us? But she had to make some compromises with my dad, and that ended with us living on the East Coast, hours away from the nearest slope. Going on this annual trip was as close as my mother was going to get to bestowing that time she loved so much onto us. I could never tell her how much anxiety the trip really caused me. Some things are just better left unsaid.

I methodically packed my carry-on bag. My mother might be insane when she packs, but I am her daughter, which means I am just as insane, if not more. I have taken every ounce of her insanity and then some.

Packing was never something that was a big deal to me until I got to middle school. When I was younger, my parents would always pack for me. The first time I ever packed for myself was not on a ski trip. I think my mom might've had an aneurysm if my first time packing had been for one of our ski trips. I still don't know how she would have handled that. We were going on a beach trip down to Florida for a week. I knew I was supposed to get my period. I had gotten it a few months beforehand and never really had that period of time where my period wasn't regular. It always has been, and until I decide to get pregnant (if I decide to get pregnant), it always will be. Yet the fact that I was supposed to get my period the day we were flying down to Florida simply slipped my mind. And not in the way of not packing any pads with me for the flight (I hadn't been using tampons back then), I didn't pack them at all. I didn't realize until we were getting on the plane and some nice lady came up to us and let me know I had bled right through my pants. I don't think I've ever seen my mom so furious. Her face turned bright red as she quickly wrapped a sweatshirt around my waist and tried to figure out how much time we had before we would be boarding so that she would be able to run to one of the nearby shops in the airport and buy me a pack. It was an emergency like no other.

I guess she has always been a helicopter parent, though. She was just always there. She worked from home and was able to be on top of my sister and me no matter what we were doing. From homework to extracurriculars to college applications, she was standing over me, watching what I was doing as if one wrong move was going to screw everything up, as if I was going to screw everything up. It's scary having a mother who checks your grades on the online portal more than you do. I swear, the second a teacher puts a grade into the grade book, she gets a notification. And if that grade is anything less than stellar, please pray for me. I will need it.

I don't want to say she scares me; she obviously doesn't and clearly has been doing some things right. I am waiting to hear back from some of the top schools in the country, I'm at the top of my class, and I have a relatively nice social life. To her, I'm the perfect daughter. The daughter she always wanted. The daughter she knew my sister would never be. And that was always part of the problem, but even she is too self-absorbed and obsessed with how everyone else sees her to wonder if that might have anything to do with my sister's death. In reality, we don't know; there was no suicide note, nothing. All I do know is the fact that Evangeline knew she would never be the daughter her parents wanted was eating her up inside and tearing her apart. She was working as hard as she could, but she was never going to be good enough. She was never going to be what our parents wanted. It didn't matter how much time she studied; she still wouldn't get the same grades I did. She asked to be evaluated for a learning disability. Her elementary school teachers had tried to bring that very topic up to my parents, but they were too stubborn to want to think that their daughter might need help, that she might be different. And her struggles with learning, and the way her teachers had to help her, was what caused her to be bullied. She probably hated it just as much as my parents did, but in all fairness, there was nothing she could do to get them to change their minds. They weren't going to be the parents of a disabled child, and therefore she wasn't allowed to get the help she rightfully deserved.

But where she lacked in academics, she excelled in sports. She was the best soccer player in our entire school. In high school, that gained her some popularity. It was well deserved, and no one was as proud of her as I was, but at the same time, she couldn't get past the bullies from her younger years. She couldn't bear to be in the same social circles with those very people, and soon she decided it wasn't worth it for her. She just kept her head down, did her work, went to practice, and tried her best. I was always so proud of her. I wished my parents were able to see what an amazing person she was. I couldn't have asked for a better sister.

I put the last item into my carry-on and sat down on my bed, then scrolled through the notifications on my phone. As expected, there were at least a dozen texts in the group chat I had with my two best friends.

> KYLE
>
> Party at Mari's tonight?
>
> TAYLOR
>
> Hell yeah!
>
> Theme???
>
> KYLE
>
> idk you text her
>
> TAYLOR

Mari said no theme :(

Someone pls tell me what to wear.

Maybe my new blue top and jeans

KYLE

why does it matter what you wear

TAYLOR

Aubrey??? You there???

KYLE

We know youre lurking bestie youre not
getting out of this.

TAYLOR

it's senior year!!! Come get drunk with us!

Pleeeeeeeeeease

KYLE

you don't have to drink. Taylor stop
pressuring her. But please come.

I sighed and flopped onto my bed. Parties weren't typically my scene, but we all have to make sacrifices for our friends from time to time. If I didn't, I'd be a really shitty friend. So, I did pop in when I felt I had to, especially if my friends were hosting, but if I could avoid it, I would. I wanted nothing more than to be able to avoid the party and just have a chill night in my bedroom alone, but I knew my friends wouldn't let me. They would show up at my house and physically drag me if they had to.

sorry I was packing.

youre not letting me get out of this one
are you?

TAYLOR

it's senior year!!! We should be partying!!!!

KYLE

it shouldn't be too many people us the rest of
the band and maybe like 10 others

TAYLOR

hahahha everyones talking about it already
not gonna be so small anymore

KYLE

it wont be that bad I promise. I stay with you
the whole time

> fine ill go but if im miserable you owe me hot
> chocolate for the whole week.

KYLE

sounds unfair

> youll each get my hot chocolate for half
> the trip

> sounds fair to me

KYLE

want me to come pick you up?

> nah, Maris close ill walk

I knew that in my current state, there was no way I was going to be able to brave this party. Going out like this, dressed up with the perfect amount of makeup on, has always been a defense mechanism for me. The Aubrey who is dressed normally can't face everything this elevated Aubrey can. She can go to a party without being overly anxious if she doesn't have a drink in her hand. She has this confidence that I wish I had in my little toe. It's like a disguise that I can put on and be the person that I wish I could be.

Yet I have to take the time to turn into that version of

myself. It takes more makeup than I would typically want to wear, but that's fine. It's like my shield of armor. My hands were trembling as I began the lengthy process of applying the makeup. In the last six months, my anxiety has gotten exponentially worse, though it's not like anyone around me might have actually noticed. I've always thought I was pretty good at hiding it and keeping my cool facing outwards, but lately, it's gotten harder to hide. Lately, it's taken all of my energy to not be in one constant panic attack.

It's funny how my friends don't see it. I guess I've been pretty good at hiding it because they see the same person that they hang out with, but here's the catch: I act one way with my friends and the people I trust and another way with those that I don't know as well. And I'm a different person when I'm with my family as well! My family doesn't always get to see my chaotic side, as I like to think about it at least. My friends have seen me in my weirdest moods at two in the morning, and my parents would never get to see that part of me.

The walk to the house wasn't all that long. It was just a few houses down from mine. It was so close I didn't even think to take a jacket. It probably wasn't warm enough for me to be outside without a jacket, but the walk was quick enough that I didn't even notice the cold nipping at every single bit of exposed skin.

I walked into the house and anxiously looked around for a drink. The place was familiar. I wasn't entirely sure which of my classmates lived here, but they hosted parties like this more than most. The house was incredibly crowded and full of people. Too full. It was like everywhere I went, I was surrounded. There wasn't an inch of free space in the entire house. I began to feel as though I couldn't breathe. The room was closing in on me, and I was all alone. I had no one to come save me. No one to make me feel safe. I searched for my friends among the crowd, but we had all come separately. I felt my heart begin to race as I realized they weren't anywhere near me. I tried to focus on my breathing. I needed to stay calm. I needed to be able to just stay focused in the moment. But I felt so lost. I felt as though I was reaching for the next rung on a moving ladder, like I was going to fall at any moment. I felt as though I was swatting at the air as I fell, hoping to be able to grab on to something to stop my fall, but my breath quickened, and I began to shake. I needed to find a seat. I needed to sit down. I was going to pass out if I didn't, and isn't that a fun way to start a party. I could barely see three feet in front of me and was navigating through the building on muscle memory alone, which wasn't the brightest idea considering how little I had been in the space.

I slowly walked to the emptiest corner I could find, yet it was still incredibly full of people, and sat with my back up against the wall. I was in this weird state between feeling trapped and working on calming down. I closed my eyes and hoped no one would bump into me or step on me. I began to shake harder and harder. It was as if there was nothing I could do to control my own body.

"Hey, you don't look so good. I got you some water. I hope that's okay." I heard a voice above me pulling me out of my trance. I looked up to see a tall redhead holding a bottle of water out to me. She was absolutely beautiful. Her green eyes were warm, and she looked so familiar.

I smiled and accepted the water. In return, she sat down next to me. I should have thought this was odd. I mean, it was. No one just comes up to you at a party with water and sits with you. At least not here.

"I'm not a huge fan of these kinds of parties either," she said with a smile. For the first time since I walked into the house, my breathing began to slow to a normal pace. "I'm Perri, by the way."

Her smile lit up the entire room. She was this bright ball of energy, but in the calmest way possible. "Aubrey," I nearly choked out as I tried to alternate between gulping down the water and drinking at a normal pace.

"I should have known," I felt my face grow warm and red at her words. Was I really that popular? "My cousin Kyle talks about you nonstop. You'd think he's obsessed with you by the way he talks about you."

My best friend's cousin. No wonder she was being so nice to me. I wouldn't have expected it from anyone else except my friends themselves. Sometimes I don't even understand why they are friends with me. It feels as if I'm always causing problems for them. If it wasn't for them, everyone at school would probably look at me like the weirdo with no friends that no one cares about. I even wonder if Taylor is being forced to be friends with me. Recently, I feel like she's always been really detached and doesn't seem to want to spend much time with me. She seems to feel distant when we're talking, and it's been beginning to feel like she doesn't have time for me. It's not something I should be too worried about, I know. If I was her, I'd probably do the same thing. I wouldn't want to be friends with me. I don't think there's anyone that should want to be friends with me, honestly. I'm just a boring, anxiety-ridden mess who seems to fuck up everything she gets.

I wish I were cool. I wish I were able to stand in front of my friends with the biggest smile on my face, in full confidence that they love me for who I am, nothing more and nothing less. Yet, I'm somehow always convinced that they are only around because they have to. I know friendships are two-sided and that both of us have to put in the effort, but I always wonder what would happen if I stopped. If I didn't text them for a few days, would they text me? Would they notice? Or would I just go unnoticed? Or might they even be happy to have a break from me? Might they just need that little reprieve to be able to take a break from the act.

But Perri's words rang through my mind: "it's like he's

obsessed with you." I couldn't seem to find my way past that. It struck me as weird. I could never picture the Kyle that I have grown to know and love being obsessed with me, talking about me all the time as if I was the greatest person to walk the earth. The funny thing is, I'm not. I'm just a boring, anxious mess trying to find her purpose in this world. I'm just trying to get by.

"I guess Kyle didn't tell you yet." She looked toward the ground and began to play with the cuff of her jacket. "I'll be joining your ski trip this year." She didn't lift her gaze. "My parents are going through some stuff, and they want me out of the house while everything gets settled. Guess there's nothing easier than being able to send their daughter away for a week, right?" She laughed, and there was a deep sadness behind it. But I barely knew this girl; I couldn't logically ask her much about it.

But it was oddly calming how much she reminded me of Kyle. I mean, it makes complete sense since they are related and all, but he's normally the one to find me when I'm in this kind of state. He's the one that will talk to me and pull me out of it, but now he's nowhere to be seen. I guess I should let him enjoy this party too. This is his last pre-winter break party in high school, and soon enough we'll all be going our separate ways. He deserves to have a moment with all of his friends. With all of our classmates. We all deserve this.

However, talking to Perri was almost more calming. There was something in her tone of voice that wasn't there when Kyle tried to be gentle with me. All of a sudden, Kyle and Taylor appeared, towering over us in our little corner. We hadn't gotten up off the ground, at least not yet. The two of them had the biggest, goofiest smiles on their faces, and I could feel everything shift into place. They were drunk. Very drunk. It's not like they don't drink, but they normally don't drink that much. But judging by their stance, it became clear to me that they had more to drink than usual. I felt a pang of jealousy as I saw them being able to relax and have fun so easily. Why couldn't it be like that for me?

"Good thing the two of you are getting along," Taylor slurred as she took another sip of her drink. She turned to Kyle and almost started laughing as she attempted to whisper into his ear, "Our plan is working perfectly."

"What plan?" Perri spoke up before I got the chance. I knew I wasn't going to be able to find the courage to ask, so I was relieved when she was able to ask for me.

"Well, Perri, if you ski with Aubrey all week then Kyle and I get to go off and ski the harder stuff without worrying about her. It will be just like when Evangeline would ski with us, and I'll finally get to have some fun."

Taylor's last sentence was a punch to the gut. Though I still felt faint, I stood and tried to make my way to the door as tears flooded my vision. I just needed to get home.

"Kyle, this has got to be some fucking joke," Perri said as I made my way out of the room. "I thought we were actually going to get to spend some time together. I thought you'd actually be on my side this time! It's been a year since I last got to see you, and you just want to dump me with your friend?"

"Perri, that's not what I meant. But you're so good at teaching and so kind, and I just want to ski the hard shit. You get to ski all year; I only get the one week." Perri just started laughing, and I was honestly shocked to hear it.

"We'll revisit this later, when you're sober. And can we go home? Have you had your fun?"

I just turned and left, unable to listen to any more of the conversation. Clearly, my friends just didn't want to spend time with me. And when I closed the door and began to walk down the sidewalk so late at night, I was even more hurt to see no one following me. I was especially hurt that Taylor wasn't there. For the first time since Evangeline's death, Taylor wasn't right by my side. Maybe I've been putting too much pressure on her to be the friend I need in a time of crisis, but the comfort that I've been relying on her for was lost in the void of a drunken teenage party. What a way to start my last winter break of high school. I guess it couldn't get worse from here, right?

Chapter Two

When we all got to the airport, it was clear that both Kyle and Taylor were hungover. At least someone had a good time last night. It was pretty early in the morning, so I don't blame us for all being virtually silent as we ate breakfast in the airport, but I wasn't getting past what Taylor said last night that easily. I want to, though. I really want to. I want to be able to excuse his actions and move on and go back to how things were. I wish it was that easy.

I can see it clearly from her perspective. We used to be a group of four. And I know he wasn't as close to Evangeline as I was. No one was as close to her as I was. But I can't ignore the fact that we're all still grieving, and that this being the first trip without her isn't going to be easy on any of us. But does that excuse her actions? No. Words carry weight, and those were some heavy words she threw at me.

I wish I could say this was the first time I experienced anything like this with Taylor, but I would just be lying. I mean, we've always fought like sisters, but recently she's just been more distant. Like in every way imaginable. She's been my best friend since we were born, yet I can barely even get through to her. It's as if she doesn't want to be around me anymore.

I've always loved getting breakfast at the airport, especially before an early flight. It's always felt like a little treat, like the start of the vacation. But this morning, the last thing I wanted to do was have to sit at a table with Kyle, Taylor, and Perri. Normally, I would appreciate that our parents want to put the four of us at a table together. Normally, I wouldn't want to pass up an opportunity to spend time with my best friends.

"So, what's everyone most excited about?" Kyle asked after we ordered our food in an attempt to start a conversation.

"Well, I was looking forward to spending time with you," Perri snapped. "But clearly you have other plans."

Taylor sipped on her coffee and smirked. "I'm excited to head up 9990."

Kyle's face lit up at the mention of one of the only ski lifts on the mountain that leads to exclusively black diamond runs. "Oh, I really hope it's open! We didn't get to go up there last year."

"Sounds really fun! Kyle, I thought you'd be showing me all of your favorite runs. Maybe you'll take me up there at some point," Perri said eagerly.

"Good luck getting Aubrey up there," Taylor said under her breath, and I felt Perri deflate beside me.

"I was looking forward to spending some time in Dolly's," I said quietly, though no one probably even cared. "It's weird without Evangeline here."

Kyle's face softened, and he reached across the table to grab my hand, but I pulled my hands into my lap before he could grab it. Just as an awkward silence fell over the table, the waiter made his way over with our food, and we all dove in without a second thought.

It's weird to think of how many memories we have in just this airport alone. It feels almost silly to think about. Airports are just a stop on the way from one place to another, yet they hold almost as many memories as the trips themselves. I can point out the seats I sat in with Evangeline when I got my period for the first time in the airport. And the seats from when she got hers. It became almost like a rite of passage or tradition for us.

It's not like we spend a lot of time in airports. We travel a couple of times a year, but at nearly eighteen years old, I can't remember a time when we weren't in an airport at least four to six times a year. Maybe that's just me and my family. There have been years when I have spent more time in the airport, especially when we would go visit my grandparents before they moved to be closer to us. But this is the first time without Evangeline. It's only been six months since she passed, but that seems to feel like forever. It's weird. Sometimes I feel as if our relationship and the sister I knew were just figments of my imagination. It's a weird thought, but as we move farther from those moments, all I have left are pictures, videos, and memories. Yet, I feel like my memory fades every day.

I would give almost anything to go back to the moment when I got my period, sitting two gates down from where we are now. I was scared and had already bled through my new jeans, but I wish I could see the smile on Evangeline's face again. To her, it was the funniest thing. I was so mad at her for laughing at the time. Who wouldn't be? I was so embarrassed and couldn't wait to get to our destination so I could change out of my blood-stained pants. I'd give anything to have her laugh at me again. I miss the way her eyes used to light up as she laughed. I miss her smile and the way she used to laugh. Really, I miss everything about her.

While waiting at the gate, I cracked open one of the many books I was bringing with me on the trip. I was sitting next to Perri, and she just sat there glued to her phone. When she did look up at me or Kyle, she had this grimace on her face, a look of pure disgust, that wiped away any thought of engaging. I was going to have to spend the whole week with her, and even though I wasn't thrilled about it, she seemed completely miserable.

We began to board the plane, and I was glad to get some separation from Kyle and Taylor. But I felt as though I couldn't keep my eyes off Perri. She looked so out of place among the group. She looked as if she was doing all that she could to fit in without being able to do just that. She wanted to, it was clear, she wanted all of this to be an extravagant trip and a getaway from the mess that was her current home life, but she had stepped right into the mess that is ours. I wouldn't be happy either. I bet she feels like a pawn in some sick game her cousin is trying to play. A game she doesn't know the name of. All she knows is that she's supposed to play the role of the dead girl's replacement by spending time with her grieving sister so her cousin can go and have fun. Because worrying about me is not fun. Because no matter what he tells me, I will always be a burden. No matter what he tells me, he really doesn't want me there. He wants someone else to have to deal with me. He wants a break from me.

There's always been a part of me that worried that my anxiety was too much. I worry that the people who are meant to love me the most end up hating me because I'm too much to deal with. I never want to be the friend you have to tiptoe around to be able to speak to. But somehow, I became that friend. I became the friend that everyone is far too cautious around because, God forbid, they say the wrong thing. Who knows what could happen to me? For all they know, I could end up like my sister. That's really what everyone's scared about. I'm the dead girl's sister. I'm the sister of the girl who killed herself before I could get there to make sure she was okay because I was far too overwhelmed with schoolwork. The only difference people see when it comes to the two of us now is that I somehow don't "have the guts" to do what she did. Or maybe they think I'm stronger than her for braving this world without her.

No one tells you how fucked up it is to bury your younger sister. Nothing can prepare you for the pain and the grief that follows. Nothing could have prepared me for the looks I get when I go out into the small town I live in because everyone knows. They read about it in the paper and then said things like "what a tragedy" and had conversations with their children about how it's okay to not be okay and taught them how to ask for help if they need it. My sister became a lesson. She became the name of a sports scholarship created by my school. But all in all, she's just another body in the ground, a headstone in the graveyard, and a sister gone too soon.

When I was growing up, I was always told that "things are replaceable, people aren't," but I don't think that really made sense to me until I lost my sister. And even now, on this first trip without her, it has solidified. Because I'm sure Perri's a really sweet girl. She seems kind and she's my best friend's cousin, but she will never replace Evangeline. And I know Kyle didn't mean it like that. I know he was drunk and said something he didn't really mean in the moment and, honestly, he probably doesn't even remember that he said it, but the fact that he said it still hurts because I know he knows how to hurt me when he needs to. He knows me inside and out, and if he really wanted to hurt me, it wouldn't be hard for him to do just that. He knows each and every flaw and insecurity I have. He had so much to choose from if he wanted to hurt me, so why that?

Finally, after a flight that felt like it would last forever, we landed in Salt Lake City, Utah. I was eager to get off the plane and run through the maze that is the airport so that I could feel the cold Utah air hit my cheeks. I could feel it in a way that I can only describe as home. It is nothing other than this sense of home.

I put the book I had been reading in my bag and turned to where Evangeline would normally be sitting to tell her the weirdest word I had found in the book—a tradition we always had when it came to long flights—and I felt my chest grow tight as I realized that she wasn't right there beside me. For the hours that we had been on the plane, I had become so engrossed in the book that I was reading that I had been completely pulled from reality. I had forgotten that she wouldn't be there when I was pulled from the fluffy romance novel sitting at the bottom of my bag.

Instead, when I turned, I found Perri in her seat. Of course, we couldn't have planned it better. Taylor calls her Evangeline's replacement, and then she goes and sits in the seat that Evangeline would have sat in if she got the chance?

Maybe I'm nitpicking, though. I shouldn't be so tough on Taylor. Evangeline was her friend too. She's grieving too. And maybe I shouldn't be giving Perri so much shit for something she has no control over. It's not like she wants to be in this situation either.

I'm in my favorite place in the world, my sister's favorite place in the world, and I am miserable. I am the one in control of my emotions. That's something I've been working on in therapy. My parents got so scared after Evangeline killed herself that they nearly forced me into therapy to make sure I wouldn't do the same thing. It's a little crazy, but the crazy is all worth it. I think it's been helping with my anxiety. Though I'm also not sure I see much of a difference. But I'm bad at noticing those things.

I want this trip to be a good trip. I want this trip to be a fun week. All we've got is one week. I'm going to have to make the most of it.

When our parents finally gave us some free time at the hotel to hang out, after everything was unpacked and each family was settled in their condo for the week, I made my way through the condo to my room purely on muscle memory. Well, the room I used to share with Evangeline. But now it's smaller. It's the condo Kyle normally stays in, and there's only one bed. Kyle's in the condo we used to stay in so Perri can have her own bed.

Kyle followed me into the room, almost dragging Perri and Taylor behind him. "Can we talk about this morning, please?" he asked, sitting on my bed, effectively backing me into a corner. What was I supposed to do? There was no way I was going to be able to get even a second of time to myself, even if I tried.

"I don't know what there is to talk about," I said, maneuvering my suitcase into the corner of the room where it would stay for the week. "You've said everything already."

"Aubrey come on,"

"Kyle, please, I don't want to hear it. It's the first vacation since my sister died, and my own friends don't even want to spend time with me. And you know what, I always thought you'd be the one to be right by my side no matter what, but sure, unload me onto your cousin like I'm a problem. I'm sure she's just as thrilled."

"Aubrey, that's not at all what I meant by that. She's a ski instructor."

"Oh, so that makes it better?"

"Aubrey, seriously? Why are you making such a big deal out of this? You remember what happened two years ago, he's just trying to make sure that doesn't happen again," Taylor added.

I sighed and turned to Perri, who stood awkwardly in the corner of the room, looking completely out of place. "I'm so sorry that their solution to my pain is forcing you to spend the week with me instead of them doing what would probably be a smarter idea and having the four of us ski together as a group. And I'm sorry that you have been put in the middle of all this. I'm sure this is the last thing you wanted. Now if my friends could be so kind and just let me unpack in peace since they clearly don't want to spend time with me anyways."

I turned and shakily made my way to my suitcase, hoping they would all just leave. Luckily, they took the hint and left me to unpack alone. As I began to unpack, I couldn't help but think about how maybe I was just losing everyone I loved and Taylor was going to be next. I wanted to forgive her; I really did. We've been through so much, she knows so much, how can I even think about losing that? However, she still said those very words. Whether it had registered to her that it would impact me in such a way or not at the time, she let those words come out of her mouth. I will still say I forgive her, at least to myself. I want to so badly. But I know it will take more time than that. I've been struggling for months, even longer really, and the people who were supposed to be there for me just haven't been. For years I believed that she didn't want to have to deal with my anxiety, or maybe it's always been my anxiety telling me that, but by what she said. The words that so easily rolled off her tongue as though she didn't even have to think twice hit that very nerve. For years I've thought that through my anxiety alone I was keeping her from enjoying herself. Keeping her from having the most fun she could have at any place at any given time. And she basically told me I had been right. Did she mean it? Probably not. But there's this thought in the back of my mind now that every time we would be skiing with Evangeline, she would take over that part of comforting and taking care of me so that Kyle and Taylor could have fun because that was technically her job. As my sister, that was her job whether she wanted it or not. She probably hated it too. She probably never wanted to have to take care of her older sister. That was always supposed to be my job. But my anxiety got in the way and it became her job too. We took care of each other. I couldn't help but always feel like I was holding everyone back. Everyone would have to sit and wait for me to get through whatever it was I was going through in that moment.

And it's not like Kyle's much better, but maybe somewhere deep down, he does feel ever so slightly guilty about leaving me and his cousin stranded. Sure, I'm not the best person to ski with. I get that, but I guess I always thought Kyle would have my back. I always thought he'd be here for me through absolutely everything. And them bringing Perri into this, like, that's his cousin. His family. I'd think he'd be dying to spend time with her, though to be fair, I don't know much about their relationship.

It's weird how much losing my sister feels like I've lost the most important job of my life. One second, I was someone's sister. I was the older sister. The person she could look up to and go to when she needed help. The next I was burying my sister knowing that I was going to have to come to terms with the fact that I was now an only child.

It's weird how much being here reminds me of her. I can walk around for hours and think of memories and little things that happened at almost every inch of this place. I can tell you where we were sitting in the Red Pine Lodge when soda came out of her nose for the first time, or what hot chocolate was her favorite from Murdock's, even though she had to try every single one every year as if they would somehow change. Hazelnut was always her favorite, but she'd never listen if I tried to tell her that. She would always try them all, claiming it was "tradition."

Chapter Three

I grabbed a cup of hazelnut hot chocolate from Murdock's as I walked back to the hotel. We would need to pick up our rentals soon, and I wasn't prepared to be back in ski boots again. They are probably the most painful shoes a human can willingly wear, other than heels, that is, but I will wear either when the occasion calls. Though it does make me wonder if women just like pain. I don't, but I guess I've learned to deal with it to make myself look appealing. Though there's never anyone I would want to impress.

I walked back into the hotel room to find my parents sitting on the couch in the living room. The TV was on, but I could tell they weren't really paying attention. My mom's eyes were glossed over, and my father looked to be nearly asleep. They didn't turn when I opened the door, or even say anything as I walked past them with my steaming cup of hot chocolate. This was hard for all of us. That was just the nature of the trip. The room was dripping with memories and moments; how could any of us really feel okay?

Picking up rentals is one of my least favorite parts of arrival day. It's tedious more than anything, but carrying skis in general has always been something I've hated. It's the one part of skiing I could do without.

We get in line at the rental place. It's the same place we go to every year, yet this year the line feels longer as it snakes around the building. The twelve of us do end up making up a large chunk of the line. Our parents talk, Taylor's brothers seem to be lost in their phones, and the four of us stand in an awkward silence. We watch people walk to and from across ski beach. The colorful jackets feel like a blur against the white background.

"Two out of ten." I hear Kyle say as he comes up behind me, pointing at a girl in a navy-blue coat. "It's just basic. We've seen it before."

I smile inwardly. The stupid game we've been playing since we were little kids, of course, would be coming back out in a moment like this. It was crazy how the smallest little comment would make me want to cry.

"Now that's a ten out of ten," I said with a smile as I pointed to a girl in a bright pink coat with a rainbow stripe going across the jacket.

Kyle and I started playing this game the first time we skied together. We were on the Saddleback lift, and it had stopped. Normally, when a lift stops for a little bit, I can handle it, but it seemed to stop for longer. My anxiety started to take over, and even Evangeline didn't know what to do in that moment. She seemed stumped as to how to help me. But then Kyle pointed at a skier down below us and asked me what I thought of their jacket. It was a simple gesture, but it said much about Kyle's character. He distracted me like no other. Since then, it's the easiest way for him to tell me he thinks I'm anxious or his way of telling me he can tell something's off. It's so simple. I honestly find it to be somewhat funny since it is rooted in us judging others, but it's in a way that we feel we can justify. It's not like we are going up to every person that we are judging and telling them their jacket is basic. If we're lucky, we'll be able to tell someone whose jacket we love that we think it's really cute, but even that rarely happens.

Perri looked over at us laughing, and it was as if a dark shadow was cast over her face; as if there was a storm brewing deep inside her brain. I couldn't help but go quiet, trying my best to focus on anything other than my friend standing next to me.

Kyle kept looking over at me as if he wanted to say something but didn't know what. "Did you see how much snow they got last night?" Kyle asked the group. I could see that he was trying, trying so hard, but I just couldn't engage as if everything was normal.

Eventually, my family got to the front of the line. First, we were asked if anything had changed from the information that had been in the computer since last year. My dad tried to make a joke about how there were four of us last year, and three of us this year, but it fell flat. That was the biggest change. The real change. Sure, we all change from year to year, but nothing magnifies that like losing someone.

We were told where to sit, and someone came over with boots that were supposedly the size we had worn the previous year.

Ski boots are one of the worst inventions to exist. We're told to wear the boots as tight as we can, but if they're too tight, you can hurt yourself. If they're too loose, you might also hurt yourself. And no matter how tight or loose they are, they're not comfortable. You can't tell if they fit just by putting them on. That would be far too easy. But you can't tell by walking around in them either. Walking isn't going to tell you how the boots are going to feel once you're actually on the mountain. To make sure the boots fit perfectly, you put them on, stand up, and then get into a squat-like position. The position you're supposed to be in while skiing, well, if you have perfect form that is. You're supposed to lean forward in the boot as best you can. If it felt as though the boots were crushing your toes, now your feet should have slid back enough for them to be more comfortable. Well, they probably shouldn't be crushing your toes when you put them on to begin with. If they are doing that, maybe say something because they're probably a size too small.

People who ski on a regular basis (more like weekly than once a year) will probably want to buy a pair of boots that are a size too small. That smaller size will help them ski better, but if you are like me and only do it for a week, then you probably want to wear something close to your average shoe size. By doing that, you are less likely to get hurt by wearing the boot. That is, if you make sure there is nothing there other than your sock in your boot while you are skiing. I have learned from experience that when your undergarments get into the boot, it can cause you to bruise your calf muscle, and then once you sit down, you might not be able to get back up or put any pressure on it because you are in so much pain. It's not fun. I don't recommend that. Wear your equipment properly.

Once we decide that we have the right boots for the week, we move on to skis. The nice thing about going to the same rental place every year is that they always keep your length of ski on file. So, I never need to know the number because, as far as I'm concerned, I haven't grown in the last year and should be using the same length of ski. It was also very helpful when I had an instructor tell me I needed to get a longer ski. He said it would help me ski better, and he was the professional, so I took his word for it. After all, he was supposed to make me better than I was at the start of the week.

I'm glad that the rental place has all of our information in the computer from years past because if they didn't, I'm not sure I'd be getting the same equipment I've gotten in the past. I would be far too scared to actually say anything about the equipment I was using, even if I knew it wasn't quite right. That's just how I tend to function.

But once we have secured our rentals, we are then tasked with what I have deemed to be one of the hardest parts of the trip. Maybe it's just me and my weird preferences, but there's something about carrying skis that just never feels quite right. My hands are too small for me to be able to just hold my skis in one hand and my poles in the other. I can hold the binding to lift up the skis, but it puts my arm in such a weird position that I never feel like I can do it for that long. I'm not strong enough to be able to carry the skis over my shoulder. It's too difficult for me. But this time, I also have to worry about carrying my ski boots. The Velcro straps that goes across the front of both boots are stuck together so I can throw the boots over my shoulder, but I still have to get my skis and poles over to the valet.

Normally, Evangeline would grab my skis, and I would take her poles. It was such a small gesture, but it was always one that made my trip easier. It wasn't even something we would really have to think about. It would just happen. Now, I walk back to the hotel carrying all of my equipment and struggling to do so. I wish Evangeline were here. I miss her and the jokes she used to make about the equipment in our hands. It would make the walk, which always felt long with the equipment in our hands, feel pretty short.

But now, that walk seemed to drag on forever. I just wished more than anything to have my sister with me. She was the person who kept me sane in the hardest of moments. She was the one who could pick me up from the hardest of moments.

After the five minutes that felt like an hour, carrying my

skis back to the hotel so we could check them in at the ski valet, I was ready to crash. It was the first moment that I had actually gotten to myself since we had arrived here. I pulled my book out of my bag and began to read. Anything to take me out of this world for just a few minutes. I just needed some sort of escape. I just needed something.

Chapter Four

Every year on the night we arrive, we get burgers. It feels as though it's been something we've done all my life. I don't think I can remember a trip where we didn't take up half the tables at Drafts at the very early time of 4:30. It was the same number every year, twelve of us. Never more and never less. Yet even without Evangeline, we are still twelve. It comes out almost naturally when we get to the hostess. There's a slight moment of counting, double-checking if you will, to make sure there's still twelve of us. It feels weird being the same large group of people with one of us missing. It truly doesn't feel right. There should be thirteen.

We sit at the same table we always do. Throughout dinner, it begins to feel as though nothing has changed. It's like we're back where we were a year ago. A group of twelve. Happy. Smiling. Singing far too loud and annoying anyone who tried to step foot into the restaurant. Our parents were drunk; they normally don't get this drunk when we go skiing, but every year they seem to forget how the altitude will impact them. Every year, I drink more water than I should to avoid altitude sickness. It feels weird without Evangeline right next to me, making fun of me every time I go to the bathroom. "You have to go again?" She'd always say with a sigh. "What am I going to do with you on the mountain? You know we won't be able to stop this much while skiing. You can go pee in the woods if you'd like, but don't get caught. I'd actually like to be able to ski with you for the whole trip." I'd flip her off in return and lock myself in the bathroom for the fourth time that day. We didn't need to talk about it beyond that.

If I just closed my eyes, it would feel as though nothing has changed, but even still, I can tell the person sitting next to me is not my sister. It's simply in her presence next to me, down to the way she breathes.

"Kyle, it looks like 9990 will be open tomorrow," Taylor said, looking up from her phone for the briefest of seconds. "Want to head up there early? Not that I think there's going to be a ton of people up there, I just can't wait to get up there!"

Kyle looked over to Perri and me as if he was trying to gauge our reactions. "You're not nervous about not having skied for a year? Don't you want to get back into it first?" He sounded nervous, though I couldn't tell if it was due more to the fact that Perri and I were sitting right there or actual nerves.

"Look, if you don't want to come with me, I'll go by myself. I just thought we had agreed to try and ski every open black run on the mountain. You did say you were going to do it with me this year. Especially after you chickened out last year. I'm just not letting you get in the way of my fun this year."

Kyle looked utterly shocked. He looked to Perri and me for guidance and with hope that someone would come to his side, but neither one of us seemed to want to come to his rescue. Luckily, that was right when our food came and that relieved any remaining tension as we all stuffed our faces.

After dinner, we all headed over to our old condo. Kyle's family's condo. It's just a condo. It is *just* a condo. Yet, that condo holds so much significance to me and my family. Years and years of memories within those few walls. Years of running around in that very room with Evangeline, Taylor, and then Kyle when we met him.

It's funny how we didn't become friends with Kyle until he joined us in middle school. This was a trip his family made yearly, just as both of ours did. We were always in Park City at the same time every year, yet we didn't meet him until he joined us at school. The first year his family joined us, it wasn't intentional. We had barely been friends at that point. We hadn't even been in school together for a year, but when Taylor and I ran into Kyle over at ski beach the excitement that overcame us was palpable. It's almost as if that trip solid-ified our friendship.

Every few years, we get lucky enough to be on this trip during Chanukah. Sometimes we're only here for a small part of the eight-day holiday. This is the first year that I can remember that we are going to be here for the whole week-long holiday.

The first night of Chanukah is always the most magical. So is the last night, but there's something extra special about that first night of Chanukah. When we're home for the first night of Chanukah, it's always the night that we make latkes. But here, other traditions took priority. I'm sure we'll be making them some other time in the week.

The first night of Chanukah, we say an extra prayer, Shehecheyanu. The prayer itself translates to: "Blessed are You, Adonai our God who guides the universe, for giving us life, for keeping us alive, and for helping us reach this day." We say the prayer second to the prayer over the menorah and Chanukah. Yet, Shehecheyanu is a prayer that has always spoken to me. It's one that I have always been told was special. It is a prayer of firsts. That's why we say it on the first night of Chanukah and not the other seven nights. But now, it takes on another meaning.

But singing it now as we light the candles feels weird.

More than I have in the past six months I notice the lack of Evangeline's presence. I feel heavy when I can't pick out her voice among the group. Her voice was so beautiful. She was one of the leading song-leaders. I never understood how she was able to do that. She was always so busy since she made the varsity soccer team as a freshman, but she always made time for temple and youth group. Those were the two places where she lit up, the soccer field and the bimah.

When my parents and I get back to our hotel room, we light the candles again, the three of us. Here, more than with the group, I feel the absence of my younger sister. But as we light the candles, the emptiness seems to fade. For a minute, I can feel Evangeline beside me. I can hear her singing along with me as the prayers leave my lips. I can feel her arms around my neck when I would walk into her room after a weekend away or after she would have a hard day. I can feel her tears soaking my shirt as she would cry, but failed to realize that those were actually tears of my own, flowing freely as I stood alone with the menorah, staring out the window, wondering if I had done something so utterly wrong to end up without my baby sister. Everyone always tells me it's not my fault that she's gone. I think my parents blame themselves almost as much as I do, if not more, but there's something so heartbreaking about spending such a beautiful holiday in such a gorgeous place, knowing she will never get to experience this. She would have loved this. I can't think of much that she would have loved more than lighting the Chanukah candles overlooking Park City. If there is anything she would have loved more, it might have been Havdalah outside in the snow. Maybe I'll do that for her tomorrow night.

The flames of our candles danced on our travel menorah. There was almost a disconnect between the holiday and the menorah we had brought with us. The one we use at home would be way too hard to travel with, but not using it has left me feeling empty. The delicate menorah we use at home is one that Evangeline and I made together out of clay. It is not the most stable, and every year we use it, I worry that it's about to crumble and fall apart, but after almost fifteen years, it has still held up. It's obvious why we don't travel with it, but there's something almost sad about not being able to travel with it. I just wish I could bring Evangeline with us, and that menorah is one of the few things we still have of her. One of the few things she made and left us with. She didn't even leave us with a note. She just left me with frantic texts, scared she was going to do something she would regret, and I wasn't there. When she was at her lowest, I wasn't there.

Chapter Five

I was up before my alarm on the first morning. I seem to always forget that the time change can feel really drastic when you're such a morning person. My body has become so accustomed to my 7 a.m. alarm that even on weekends, I don't seem to be able to sleep later than 8:30. But 8:30 at home is 6:30 here, so I am up before the rest of my family.

Evangeline used to get up with me. She was always a light sleeper, so the second I got out of bed, she was awake, even if she didn't want to be. We would talk in hushed tones and turn on the TV in our room with the volume as low as it could possibly go. Low enough not to wake our parents, but loud enough so that we could still hear it. It was the perfect volume. It worked nicely because even the quietest setting eventually became too loud for us.

Now it was 4:30 on a Saturday morning, and I was the only person awake. Sometimes I like being up before most people. It can feel empowering, but on mornings like these, it just feels lonely.

I went through the motions as I always would. A bowl of dry cereal to snack on, nothing too big though, I'd probably be having eggs for breakfast, and a glass of water. Always a glass of water. And then I'd turn the TV on as low as the volume could go and search for a channel. It was weird not having to argue with someone about what I wanted to watch. It was all up to me. I had about an hour before everyone would start waking up and getting ready. We'd all have breakfast in the restaurant at the hotel. Always a buffet. Always has the same food.

It almost feels like when I'm here nothing changes. Everything seems to stand still here. Year after year, memories build on top of each other yet the place stays the same. Sure, there's a new restaurant here and there every once in a while, but that's barely anything. From the outside, the buildings still look the same.

We sit at breakfast like we always have, and probably always will. Parents and adults take up the first six seats of the long table, the kids on the other half. Taylor's brothers act as our divide from the adults. They sit across from each other, just like always. They seem to barely know what's going on around them. They have their noses in their phones. Kyle and Taylor sit across from each other next to Taylor's brothers. I sit next to Kyle and across from Perri. Of course, that's where Evangeline used to sit. Where Evangeline should be sitting. The lack of her presence hangs heavy in the air yet no one else seems to notice. I'm the only one impacted by it. Time moves on as normal. Everything works as it should. Not a single thing is out of place. No one thinks to stop or take a second. My world has stopped. Everything has stopped. Yet everything is expected to move forward.

I look at the table in front of us. A family of four, just as ours used to be. A mom, a dad, and two young girls. One of the girls looks at me and smiles. I wonder what she's thinking. When she looks at me, is she wondering what her future might be, just as I used to? Or can she see the mess that I have become?

Perri smiles at me from across the table. Her smile is warm

and inviting, welcoming and calm. Yet as I look at her, I feel anything but calm. I try to focus on the details. I take in her smile and the curve of her lips, the way the skin around her eyes crinkles and puckers with the movement. The way her big eyes and long lashes make her look innocent in a place where I know she's not.

I think she's talking to me. Her mouth is moving; surely, words are coming out, but I can't seem to grasp a single one. They surround me like dust particles in the air. They float on by, but I doubt I will be able to actually catch them. I want to hang on just enough to grasp what she's trying to say.

I slowly start to make out some of the words she's saying. I only hang on to each word for a second or two. Kyle pops in to say something. I hear his voice but cannot seem to make out the words that he is actually saying. That's the only thing able to clue me in on the fact that we are having a conversation.

I guess this sort of happens sometimes. I wish it didn't. It makes functioning during times of extreme stress and anxiety very hard. But why here? Why now? I wish I knew how long this would last.

Kyle's hand eventually found my own, the simple touch pulling me back into the current moment. We were the only two left at the table. Everyone else had gotten up to get food, leaving us without me even noticing. Kyle gave my hand a little squeeze. The small gesture reminded me that he was going to be there for me.

I know Kyle will always be here for me. There's a sense of friendship that has always been between us, but it's these moments that can solidify that for me. I can get so in my head when it comes to my friends and my friendships. I can walk around saying Kyle is my best friend all day long, but when I go home and get a moment alone, do I even believe that? Or do I spend nights sitting on my bedroom floor, wondering why my friends even put up with me, wondering why they haven't given up on me, and wondering if they really love me or are just being friends with me because they feel bad for me. Because without them, who would I be, both as a person and in our school's social spheres?

We slowly made our way over to the breakfast buffet. If I'm being completely honest, nothing looked all that appetizing. I wasn't even sure I wanted breakfast. I always looked forward to eating here. I normally love breakfast food. It's my favorite food to eat, but I just felt off. I knew it would be best for me to eat something, so I filled my plate as I would normally do. The goal of the day was to make everything look normal. The last thing I wanted was to cause a scene or bring any more attention to myself. I was already dealing with enough of that.

When we sat at the table, Kyle looked at me with a worried expression on his face. This was no way for me to be starting a day, especially not our first day of skiing. I just needed to focus on the task at hand. I just needed to clear my plate. It was the first day of skiing; I wasn't going to ruin it. I already felt as though my mental state on this trip was ruining it as it was.

I picked at my food. Honestly, I couldn't bring myself to eat. I knew I needed to eat if I was going to be out on the mountain all day, but I could barely bring myself to put any food in my mouth. I forced myself to eat one of the pancakes I had grabbed from the buffet and then tried for a few strips of bacon, but I found them to be far too greasy, though that's never stopped me before.

Eventually, it was time to move on and start skiing. Our rentals were waiting for us out by the slopes, and grabbing them wasn't too difficult. I felt shaky in my ski boots. My chest was tight, and breathing was not coming easily to me. We made our way to the Orange Bubble Express and put our skis on before getting in line. It wasn't that long, luckily. I had seen it with almost a twenty-minute wait time before, but at least we were in line and on our way to getting up the mountain.

There's a level of anxiety surrounding everything I do, especially skiing. Sometimes I get on a run and I'll just freeze. It could be my first time on the run, or I could have done it 100 times, but for some reason, the conditions that day just aren't right. I start heading down the run with the intention of making my way down it, but the second I start to make my way down, it's like I've made the worst mistake. My heart starts racing, and I feel like I can't breathe. I don't know how I'm going to make it down, even if the next turn is right in front of me. I can see where I need to turn and what I need to do to make it down the run safely, but it's like my brain and my body can't connect. The more I stand there looking at the bottom of a slope, I get more and more scared. And then I start to feel like I can't do it, but I'm standing on the top of a mountain and if I don't ski down, I'll be stuck up there. I try to tell myself that I need to get down or I'll die up there, but that never seems to help. Maybe I should stop doing that. Eventually, and generally with help from an instructor, I am able to make the first turn. It's a painful turn. My form is awful as I make that first turn. Then I will slowly make my way down the rest of the run and by the end, I do feel better. There's a sense of pride that comes with making it down the run and accomplishing something that felt impossible.

But sometimes, skiing can make me feel so powerful. When I make it down those runs that plague me with that pit of anxiety in my stomach, I feel powerful. Standing at the bottom of a steep run, looking up, always comes with this overwhelming feeling of accomplishment. It feels weird to take such pride in something so small, but it's the only way that I can motivate myself to do it over and over again.

On the lift, I sit at one end, next to Kyle. Taylor is next to him, and Perri is at the other end. At moments, Perri tries to start conversations. She's trying really hard, and I can't fault her for that, but I wasn't talking. Not that anyone was surprised by my silence. But even Kyle and Taylor were oddly quiet.

Kyle had his hand placed gently over mine. It was a simple gesture. A gesture that I hadn't been expecting, but it was his way of showing me that he was here and that he cared. It's not like I would think he wouldn't care, or didn't care, if he didn't do the bare minimum to show he cared. He's always cared and hopefully always will care. But maybe this is just an act. If he really did care, he'd be spending the week skiing with me and not falling for every one of Taylor's little traps.

We finally made it to the top of the lift after a ride that felt like it would take forever. My legs feel wobbly beneath me as we start to make our way down the run. Taylor and Perri lead. I hate leading more than anything, and I know that Kyle won't let me go dead last even though I know I'm skiing way too slow for him, especially on this easy run. I know he'd never say anything, but I also know by allowing him to ski behind me, I am holding him back. It's what I'm best at. Sometimes it feels as though holding people back is all I do. I know in my heart of hearts that it's not true, but there's a part of me that can't doubt the fact that everyone feels I am holding them back in one way or another.

I ski down the run slowly, probably slower than I should. I'm sure people skiing on the mountain think I'm a beginner from my speed. I know I can ski faster. I've been skiing for most of my life; this shouldn't be so hard. Why does this feel so hard? It's like every limb feels so heavy, and I can't keep my skis parallel to make turns. It's embarrassing as I almost fall multiple times as I try to turn. What is happening to me? This never happens. I've never skied like this. I should know what I'm doing. I'm better than this, right?

The harder it gets for me to ski down High Meadow, the more I begin to panic. I know Kyle is behind me, and I know he isn't going to try and ski around me to get to the bottom as fast as he can, even though he is more than welcome to do just that. My chest starts to get tight, and it is becoming increasingly harder to breathe with every turn I make. Why is this so hard? It's only been a year. A year isn't that long. This is something I've been doing for as long as I remember. Why am I feeling like this now? I shouldn't feel like this. I should be flying down this run at one of the fastest speeds that I ski at. That would be normal. This is not normal. And now I have Kyle behind me, and I'm holding him back from being able to enjoy this run. Not that he would love to be skiing this all day because it's so easy, but he should be able to make that decision for himself. He shouldn't have to feel as though he needs to be skiing behind me in case anything happens. I don't want to be the reason he doesn't have fun on this trip. I know if I say anything to him, he will just tell me that it doesn't matter what runs he skis, it matters that he's skiing with me, but I know that's a lie. He wants to ski all the crazy black runs. He wants to go up Ninety-Nine-Ninety and do all the runs I wouldn't dare ski. But he's stuck here with me and my anxiety.

It's one thing for my anxiety to hold me and my skiing back, but for someone else to be held back by it is my worst nightmare. I'm used to it at this point. I've dealt with this my entire life, and it feels as though every year we go skiing, it gets worse. When Evangeline was here, we would be responsible for each other, and she would always push me ever so slightly. Not enough to cause panic, but enough to know that I would feel as though I got something out of the trip. But I look at the group I'm with now as I finally make it down to the bottom of the run and know that none of them are willing to do that.

Evangeline was used to my anxiety. She had lived with it almost as long as I had. To her, it was nothing. She was the first person to make jokes about it and to make fun of me for it, but it was never in a malicious way. It was always comforting when she made fun of me, well, as comforting as someone making fun of you could be.

When I finally made it down the run, I was so shaken. That's not how I ski; everyone except Perri knew that. Both Kyle and Taylor looked concerned, and I began to feel as though I had done something very wrong. I knew I had done nothing wrong, or shouldn't have done something wrong, but I couldn't stop feeling like I had just fucked up the entire trip. Was I really going to ski like this for the rest of the trip? I couldn't handle that. If I was going to ski like this for the rest of the trip, I might as well just go home. There's no point in going on this very expensive trip if I can barely make it down the bunny hill after skiing for at least thirteen years. That's just embarrassing. I can't do that all week.

None of my friends seemed to know what to do. Everyone was just shocked to see me ski like that. "Why don't we have Taylor and I go off and ski some harder stuff and Perri can take you back to High Meadow and do that again?" Kyle suggested to the group. His voice was calming and brought me back to the present moment. I didn't think I would be able to speak, so I just nodded. If I tried to speak, I was sure my voice was going to betray me. I'd probably start crying.

"We can meet at Red Pine for lunch in a couple hours," Taylor suggested as she got ready to head over to the Saddleback lift. We all agreed to meet for lunch at eleven-thirty. We watched Taylor and Kyle skate over to Saddleback, and Perri put a gentle hand on the small of my back and guided me to the long line for High Meadow.

Chapter Six

P erri and I made it onto the lift after about five to ten minutes of waiting in line. It might look like a long line, but it always moves faster than I expect. Before I knew it, we were on the lift. The High Meadow lift is one that goes way too slow for its own good. I know this is due to the fact that little children who are just learning how to ski go on it when they finally make it up the mountain. Because young children are generally taking the High Meadow lift up the mountain, there are stoppers that would go in between the legs of every person on the lift as well as between people sitting next to each other.

Perri and I were lucky not to be riding the lift with a ski instructor and a young child. I would have suggested leaving the bar up during our ride on the lift if it didn't make me so anxious not to have any barrier between myself and falling off the lift. Without the bar down, I wouldn't feel safe, and when I'm currently in an anxious state, that is the last thing we need to deal with.

"I used to be a ski coach, you know," Perri said as the chair moved slowly up the lift. "You're not going to scare me away that easily." I know she meant this to be kind. None of this was meant to be malicious. She just wanted to help. But her way of helping was also a way of judging me and my skiing abilities. Well, I know she is not trying to judge my skiing; she just wants to see how I'm skiing to figure out how to get me out of my head. She's practically giving me a free lesson for at least today, if not all week.

"I may not scare you away, but we both know neither one of us really wants to be skiing with each other anyway," I snapped back. Just like Kyle, Perri means well and is only trying to help. But I've been skiing for most of my life; I should be able to do this without the help of anyone. I should be able to do this easily. I shouldn't be having this problem. I need to get beyond myself here and just ski as I normally do. "Where do you coach?" I asked, trying to at least start a bit of a conversation.

She smiled. I had asked the right question. I hadn't fucked this up yet. "I used to teach out in Denver, but with every-thing going on with my parents, I'm not sure I'm going to get much of a chance out there this season. I think my parents want to move closer to the rest of their family."

"If you do move, I hope it's closer to Kyle and me," I said before I could even realize, but it came so naturally to me. She was rambling, and I could see the pain in her eyes when it came to discussing home. I wasn't going to push. Was that a bad idea? Should I have asked her more about her family? I guess I should support her in discussing whatever she needs to, but I shouldn't take it too far yet. We've only just met. But she did first meet me during the panic attack I was having at the party when I couldn't find my friends. But she was just being kind when she came up to me and talked to me. She knows she doesn't have to. She has and never will be respon-sible for me. No one should be responsible for taking care of me. I'm too much of a mess.

"But if you already live out here, why not just meet us here instead of flying all the way out east and then all the way back?" I couldn't help but ask, the curiosity eating away at me.

"My mom's just super overprotective, and she wanted to spend some time with her parents amidst all the chaos. But really, there was no way she was letting me fly out east alone. I tried to convince her it would be cheaper, but she didn't want to hear it."

I opened my mouth to reply just as the chair pulled into the lift. We pushed ourselves off and began to prepare to ski down. There were two ways we could go from here. Normally, I wouldn't have thought for a second about which way might be harder; I've been skiing there my whole life, and they haven't changed too much. The only thing that ever changes is the conditions of the snow. But now, I noticed that one side was ever so slightly steeper than the other. I've gone down both sides more times than I could count, but now I had to choose. My first thought was to take the less steep way down. Theoretically, it would be easier. But also, if I go down the steeper side (which isn't all that steep if I'm being completely honest), it might give me more speed and make skiing down the run easier. Well, it should help make going down the run easier. I guess it would be worth a shot.

The first few turns down the run felt too fast. It was the steepness of the small hill, but it gave me the momentum I needed. It was the little push that I needed to get me down the slope at a faster speed. I was skiing faster for sure. I was more confident than the last time I went down this very run, but even still, I was tripped up in the little things. Every sound my skis made with each and every turn I took would spook me. I was digging my poles into the snow to hold myself stable.

It took another twenty minutes for me to get down the run. It was highly embarrassing. I've been doing this all my life. Why is it difficult now?

We got in line to go do the run for a third time. The last

time I had skied High Meadow this many times, I was frustrated to be in a lesson that was so below my level. Now, this is what I'm needing. It's frustrating. I shouldn't be here. I should be skiing harder and more intense runs. I should be skiing down Chicane so I can have lunch over by Tombstone, but I can barely get down High Meadow.

"Why don't we try backing up a little bit," Perri said once we were on the lift. "We're going to go back to the basics. Pizza and french fries. We'll go back to a wedge when making turns and try to keep our skis parallel when skiing across the slope. You can just follow me right in my tracks, ok?" The sympathy in her eyes was both intoxicating and infuriating, making me want to crawl into her arms but also reminding me of how everyone looked at me after Evangeline's death.

Her suggestion was simple. Just go back to the basics. It was the right thing to do. The right decision to make. But even that felt far too hard. I had to give it a chance. I just needed to be able to get out of my head and get back to my normal self. Why couldn't I get back to my normal self? But going back to the basics did nothing other than make me feel like a child. For some weird and unknown reason, this thing that has always felt like second nature to me was harder than it had ever been.

We got off the lift and began to go down the run. I followed as close behind Perri as I could. Knowing she was ahead of me and knowing that I could lose her and get lost on this run motivated me to stay closer to her.

Perri was moving relatively slowly, and for that, I was grateful. Yet, it was clear to me that she could have been skiing down harder runs, runs that she would have more fun with, and she was stuck here with me. Not that it was the worst thing in the world, at least for me. Evangeline will never be here again. Nothing I can do will bring her back. I need to make the best of this trip. It doesn't matter what it looks like.

Toward the bottom of the run, I was starting to regain my confidence. I always saw skiing as being similar to riding a bike. Once you learn how to do it, you never forget. But when the death of your sister has led to insane bouts of what my therapist refers to as "dissociation" mixed with my ever-growing anxiety, the very basic things that I have known how to do my whole life just become hard.

I was feeling better about skiing when we got to the bottom of the run. We had about a half hour until we would be meeting Kyle and Taylor for lunch. Just enough time to go down the run once more before we would have to go in. But I was feeling ballsy. I had gotten back into my parallel turns about halfway down the run and decided to ski past the High Meadow lift.

I headed to the Saddleback lift. We only had a little bit of time before we would have to meet Taylor and Kyle for lunch, but we probably had enough time for at least one more run. I wasn't sure if I was comfortable going beyond Snow Dancer, the easiest blue run on the mountain, but it was worth a try. It shouldn't be too hard for me. It shouldn't have been, anyway. It's not like I've never been down these runs before. I've been going down them since I was a little girl. I've known these runs like the back of my hand, yet now without my sister by my side, I can barely seem to ski. But Perri's making it just a little bit easier.

My sister was never meant to be the person to carry me through life. I was the older one. I was supposed to carry her, look out for her, support her. Yet somehow, we never seemed to fit into those roles. She was the one who always supported me, carried me, looked out for me, helped me. I was supposed to support her, and I clearly had failed as an older sister, but I didn't only fail her in that way. I made her take over the role that I was supposed to take on. I unintentionally threw her into a life that was making her miserable. All I had done was hurt her and harm her as she spent all of her time trying to help me. All I did was fail her.

Perri and I got in line for the Saddleback lift. The line wasn't too long, especially for a group of two. If we had really thought about it, the singles line might have gotten us up the lift even faster, but we did want to stick together.

It's always fun trying to find different ways to entertain ourselves when we're waiting in line for the lift. The lines always look much longer than they actually end up being. The lift ride is one of my favorites. It's not much different than any other lift, really. However, the years of Mardi Gras beads and Barbie heads hanging off the trees just seem so special. They're like little gifts left for us by those who came before. Old ski poles and bras are littered through the trees. I wonder if someone has ever come to clean them out and remove them. I always assumed they would, but every time we visit, the same ones seem to still be waiting patiently for us up in those trees. It's such a small thing. No one even bats an eye at them. They're just part of how the mountain is. It's something I almost expect from the Saddleback lift, and the Saddleback lift alone. I've never paid enough attention on other lifts to even know if they have all sorts of random items littering their trees, waiting for someone to claim them as their own. I'd claim almost anything I could find in one of those trees if I had the chance. A forbidden souvenir. A small token of my love for this place, wrapped in my small ungloved hand in the freezing cold, if only for a few minutes before it would be stowed away in my pocket, waiting for its final destination.

Maybe one year, I could bring something to throw up into those trees. It wouldn't serve me very well; I'd be too scared of getting caught anyway. I'm pretty sure doing that is illegal, or at least quite close to being illegal. It's something I shouldn't be doing regardless. Even if I wanted to. Evangeline and I always used to talk about how we would bring our own little goodies to throw into the trees. She'd always joke about how we'd have to do it while there were children on the lift. Of course, that would probably get us both in trouble, but on the off chance that we didn't, we would have been the pivotal moment of a core memory for those children. I know I've never been on a lift when that has happened. I've been going on lifts for most of my life. I'd know by now. I should know, at least.

I always hate when lifts stop, but at least on Saddleback, there is something for me to focus on. The view and the little goodies in the trees almost distract me from the thoughts of the lift potentially rolling back that a ski instructor a few years back put in my head. I just have to not panic. Just don't look down. It's easier said than done. The snow looks so soft though. Maybe it wouldn't hurt too much if I were to fall.

Perri softly places her gloved hand on my arm. I take a deep breath and turn to look at her. A large smile is plastered all over her face. "Is that the head of a baby doll hanging from the tree?" she asks me while trying not to laugh.

"Do you see the Barbie?" I point to a couple of trees ahead where a Barbie has some string tied around her neck. "It's a bit morbid, isn't it?"

"In a funny way though." I laughed at that. I never thought about that being both funny and morbid at the same time. Leave it to Perri to open my eyes to what I'm missing out on.

"That's why this lift has always been one of my favorites." A smile spread across my face, and when I looked at Perri, I noticed her smile matched mine. I couldn't help but begin to giggle, though it felt rather odd. But there was just something about being near her, knowing she wasn't going to give up on me like my friends had, that had me craving this alone time with her.

And then the lift started moving again. It slowly picked up speed until we moved along at a steady pace up the mountain. Finally, I could breathe. However, as we got off the lift, anxiety started to bubble in my chest yet again. I only had one option on how to get down from here. There was only one option. I had to ski down. If I didn't, I'd just be stuck up on this mountain. The confidence I had earlier seemed to vanish. I was so confident when I got down High Meadow. Where was this anxiety coming from now? I knew better than this. It wasn't like I had never done this before.

We pulled over to the side, and I slid my hands and wrists into the straps of my ski poles. I was going the easiest way down. I was going to make it down. I didn't have a choice anyway. I had to get down. I had to get to lunch.

I took a deep breath and looked up at Perri, sitting just a few steps behind me. She smiled at me and gave me a little nod. "I'll follow your lead," she said softly, and I slowly began to make my way to the entrance of Snow Dancer. If I was lucky, I'd make it down the run in a decent amount of time.

Chapter Seven

My first turn was shaky. I was stuck in a wedge and filled to the brim with anxiety. I felt as though I couldn't fully take in enough air to take a full breath. I was sitting too far back on my skis, and the lack of my proper stance caused pain to rocket up my thighs. Every muscle in my body was tense, and I tried to breathe and make my way down the run.

My second turn was better. I was still traversing across the whole run as I made that turn, my body facing across the run instead of down it, but my wedge was becoming smaller.

By my fifth turn, I was still in the wedge, but my turns were beginning to get smaller. I remembered an instructor chastising me for my big turns and telling me I was only allowed to stick to one side of the run. I knew at the time that wasn't true. And looking back now, I wonder if that instructor was just trying to use my anxiety against me. He probably made some comments about being in the way of others and how those big turns can end with someone getting hurt. He was probably right, at least to some sense of what he had said. But shorter turns mean going faster.

By the time we were about halfway down the run, I had

found my parallel turns again. The snow was packed down tight after being groomed not too long before, and I could feel my skis making fresh tracks on the recently groomed snow. My parents always love that feeling. I've always hated it. I have always thought it sounded more like nails on a chalkboard, and it always feels more unsettling than it does nice and relaxing. I mean, there is something nice about knowing that you are the first person to be on a run for that day, but at the same time, it is anxiety-inducing in every meaning of the words. I try not to think about it when I don't have to.

We made it down the run with about ten minutes to spare. It would be easy for us to go and grab a table then. Maybe get some food and then send a text to Kyle and Taylor, giving them vague descriptions as to where we are, hoping they will be able to find us. They should be able to find us; they always do.

The Red Pine Lodge has never been my first-choice pick for restaurants when it comes to this mountain, but if I was struggling to get down Snow Dancer, there is not a chance I'd be able to make it down Chicane, even if I took the bypass. It just wasn't going to happen. That's not a problem. I honestly don't mind it all that much. But I'd rather eat the barbecue at Tombstone than I would eat chicken tenders dipped in ranch, honey mustard, or whatever else they might have this year. But food is food, and as my mom loves to constantly remind me, "food doesn't have to be good. It's fuel for your body to keep on going." I know she's right. I mean, aren't mothers supposed to always be right? But there's nothing wrong with eating food that I enjoy. I only have an issue with my dress size because you have constantly reminded me that society thinks I should be a size double zero instead of the size ten I'm currently wearing. But what can I do about it? I'm sorry I have big tits and a nice ass, I guess?

Perri sees Kyle and Taylor make their way into the restaurant and waves them over to where we are sitting. Kyle immediately claims the seat next to me and, without a word, he begins to take off his gloves, jacket, helmet, and any other item of clothing he is currently wearing that he doesn't plan on wearing while eating indoors. He has this crazy look in his eyes, and it makes me wonder if he's eaten breakfast. I'm sure he'll eat most of my fries anyway.

"So how far toward 9990 did you make it?" Perri asked when Taylor and Kyle sat down with their food.

"Well, not close enough since we had to get back here for lunch with y'all. Kyle insisted on taking Red Pine Road after we made it down to Tombstone, even though I really wanted to head over to Iron Mountain." Taylor huffed. She really did seem pissed, and I was starting to feel guilty. The chicken tender in my hand no longer looked appealing.

"I said we'd go in the afternoon. We made plans. It would've been rude to just ditch Perri and Aubrey. Besides, I actually want to spend some time with them during this trip." Kyle shot me a sympathetic smile before swiping a french fry from my plate.

Taylor just rolled her eyes and took a bite of her pizza. "Whatever. But if we don't win our challenge this year it's your fault."

Lunch went by way too quickly, and now there was another question I had to face. What the hell was going to be our next run? Was I ready to push myself even further than I had been with Snow Dancer, or is that all I can handle for today? And it's not so much as to what I can handle but more what I can struggle my way through.

At least it's just the first day of skiing. I don't need to be putting pressure on myself to ski perfectly. This trip is meant for me to have fun. But I've never been on a ski trip where I haven't had a lesson, where I haven't had the perfect form I'm supposed to have drilled into me, critiqued, and criticized. My posture and my stance are things I've grown to be far too aware of. Are my feet too far apart? Am I leaning into my boots? Are my skis parallel? Is my body pointed down the slope while my legs maneuver side to side? Why is this so difficult?

Taylor and Kyle were eager to get their skis back on and go down Chicane and get over to Iron Mountain. I just wanted to join them over that way, but the last thing I wanted to do was hold them back. I was not going to be the reason that they didn't get the chance to ski all of the runs they wanted to. I didn't want them to resent me. I'm sure Perri already resents me. She's been forced to spend time with me instead of skiing with her cousin, who she clearly wants to be skiing with. She's here with us because her parents shipped her off while they deal with their own issues, and now, she has to deal with a cousin who seems to want nothing to do with her and her cousin's sad excuse of a friend.

Evangeline would never let me feel this way. I wouldn't have to say anything, and she'd be dragging me down Chicane like it was High Meadow. If I was doing well, she might even force me to skip the bypass. Now, I can barely even look at Chicane. Even the top of it, the flat part, looks too steep. I feel quite stupid, if I'm being completely honest. The one thing that used to bring me the most joy has now covered me in a feeling of pain I don't know how to get through.

We decided to go up Saddleback again. If I were feeling up to it, maybe by the end of the day we'd be able to start making our way down Kokopelli. That might be a stretch though. Even when I'm doing my best on the mountain, Kokopelli can send me into a panic attack. But maybe it won't be bad. It's only the first half of the run that makes me anxious anyway.

We went for Snow Dancer the first time. It was the obvious choice. Maybe not the choice I wanted to make with only a few hours left in the day, but it was the choice I had to make. If it was truly up to me, we would be as far from

Saddleback as possible without sending me into some form of a panic attack.

"You seem to have no problem getting your confidence back," Perri said as the lift pulled out of the station.

"Yeah, I guess. I just used to ski so much better. I don't know why I just can't seem to now." Perri reached over and placed her gloved hand on top of mine and gave it a squeeze.

"You'll get there when you're ready."

I wished I could just get myself together and get back to the way that I skied last year. I wished I could hold onto that confidence, because I know for a fact that there is no way I'm going to be able to ski down at the end of the day, and taking the gondola down at my level is just a sign of defeat. Every other year, if I've taken the gondola down, it's because I was hurt, having a panic attack, or something else was seriously wrong. I should be able to ski down. But is it worth it to push myself?

But maybe I need to push myself. I should be able to make my way down Boomer and Echo to get down. I do like those runs. I need to stop fearing what might happen and just let it happen.

We took Snow Dancer about three more times before we wanted to discuss going down for the day. It was nearly three, and we had been out skiing since so early in the morning that we might as well go in and be done.

Our last time on Snow Dancer was quite magical. I didn't think about where I was or what I was doing; I just did it. I didn't think about how I would have to get down the run or I would be stuck up at the top of the mountain forever; I just skied down it like I always had. I skied down it as if I was a ten-year-old skiing down it for the twentieth time that week because it was one of the only things that was open. If there weren't other people on the run, I think that I might have been able to ski down it with my eyes closed.

I just felt light on top of the snow. Like I was floating

above it. Gliding down the slope. I didn't notice the heavy boots on my feet pressing deeply into my shins, causing my legs an insane amount of pain. My cheeks stung from the cold, but I didn't feel it. My hand warmers were still in my pockets.

When we got down the run, I headed toward the gondola, but instead of taking my skis off to get on the gondola, I skied right past it. I wasn't giving in to my anxiety. I wasn't letting it win. I was in control and if Perri wasn't willing to push me out of my comfort zone, I had to be.

I wish I could have seen Perri's face as I kept on skiing. She must've been so shocked, but I was determined. The Shortcut lift is one that I have a love-hate relationship with. It's a two-person lift, and somewhat fast, but it is also one of the lifts that has to go down before it goes back up. When watching it, the lift looks quite scary. However, when on it, the lift doesn't feel that bad. It just always freaks me out a little bit. But that should be the least of my worries. I am going to ski down whether it kills me or not. I'm on the lift now. I have no choice.

"So, there's a rope tow down there," I said as we rode the lift. "You're going to want to bomb down the run to make it onto the rope tow. You're going to want to hold your poles under one armpit and hold onto the rope with both hands so that it can pull you up. Just follow me if that doesn't make any sense." While Perri had probably taken a rope tow before, I always feel better about being prepared for what's to come.

We got off the lift, and I led Perri onto Boomer. The flat part at the start can be pretty boring and frustrating, but once we started to make our way onto the run itself, I was reminded of why I love this run so much. I'm not much of a speed demon, especially when it comes to skiing. But knowing there are flat parts on the run and the rope tow always puts pressure on me to go faster than I would normally go.

The rope tow is one of my least favorite parts of the run and is something I would avoid if it were possible, but unfortunately, it's not. I wouldn't have such an issue with it if people actually knew not to take their little children who don't understand the rope tow down the run. Because when the kid falls in front of me because they weren't holding on tight enough or tried to go into a wedge to slow down, I end up having to climb up that bit of the run because there is no way for me to get back on the rope tow. But that's only happened once. It's not the worst thing that could happen.

Boomer, to me, has always felt like it has steepish little pitches with flatter areas in between, and after the rope tow, it's just pretty fun and chill. I had this confidence about me when I skied down the run that I hadn't experienced yet during the week.

Perri and I stopped at the bottom of the run, right outside our hotel, and I could see the shock on her face.

"You really did that!" Perri was nearly beaming with pride. She gave me such a big hug. We brought our skis back to the valet where the hotel stored them for us and then made our way back to our separate hotel rooms to get ready for dinner.

We had a reservation at a nicer restaurant tonight, and it was a restaurant I loved, but as I was getting ready, I began to feel like I didn't want to go. There was a heaviness around every movement I made. I should have been happy. I should have been proud of what I did get to ski, but I just felt disappointed in myself for what I didn't get the chance to ski. Something was setting in, and I couldn't quite place it. I just felt heavy and slow, and I really didn't want to do anything. I moved through the hotel room in such a way that I felt like I was on autopilot and wasn't doing anything for myself. I was just going through the motions and doing what needed to be done. All I wanted to do was curl up in a ball and just shut off all the lights and pretend like the rest of the world didn't exist. But I couldn't do that. We were going out to dinner, the whole large group of us, and it was still Chanukah. It was only the second night. I couldn't avoid everything that comes with each night of Chanukah.

I almost didn't know what to do with myself. I hadn't felt like that since Evangeline had died. There was a long period of time, a few months, after her death when I could barely do anything. Knowing that I am getting to the point where it has almost been a year made this feeling more understandable. I also put more brain energy than normal into thinking about and missing her. That most definitely had something to do with it.

I remember when she died, I felt so lost and so broken. I had spent so much of my life just wanting and trying to be there for her and be the best big sister I could think to be, and I remember the only thing I could feel was just failure. I had failed her as a sister. There was something I wasn't doing because why else would she have done what she did? If I did everything right as a sister, she would be here. She would still be here.

I didn't realize I was crying and completely wrapped in my thoughts until I felt the bed dip next to me. I looked up and saw Kyle sitting next to me. I hadn't even heard him come in, but I wasn't surprised. It was pretty typical for him to come over if we hadn't seen each other for most of the day. He just wrapped his arms around me and we sat in silence for a bit. We didn't have to leave just yet; we still had a little bit of time and I was really lucky we did.

"What's going on?" he whispered after a couple of minutes. I tried to take in a deep breath, but it was just shaky. I just needed to calm myself down and try to put into words how I was feeling.

"I just really miss her," I whispered. I took another deep breath before continuing. "I just feel like I'm going backward in time because I feel so heavy and like I did when Evangeline killed herself, but now I'm here and I should be happy and living in the fact that I'm in my favorite place in the world, but all I can think about is how much I wish my sister was here with me, but I know I'm never going to get her here with me again. I'm never going to get to race her down all of our favorite runs or laugh with her at all the crazy people we see. I'll never get the chance to make new memories whether they are good, bad, or somewhere in between. I thought being here would help. I thought it would make all of this pain go away, but it's only made it worse and I don't know what to do anymore." It almost made me feel better to get it all out.

"Hey, I get that. You're at a time and place in your life where you think you should be living your best life and having the time of your life, but you're here and you feel like shit because sometimes life is just shit. It doesn't matter where you are or what you are doing; life sometimes just sneaks up on you and punches you in the face. But it is okay for you to feel everything you are feeling. You need to let yourself feel. And yeah, I know, do as I say, not as I do. I know I'm shit at letting myself feel. I know that you've watched me go through shit and just put it aside because the rest of my family needs me. I need you to not do that, okay?" He gave me a good squeeze, and I nodded.

We then both got up and made our way out of the room and into the entrance area where the whole group was waiting for us. Perri smiled at us and nodded when Kyle shot her a look that said, "I'll fill you in later." We put on our jackets, grabbed our bags, and made our way out the door.

Dinner was a blur. I tried to be present. I really did, but it was just so hard for me to stay present and here throughout dinner. The world moved around me, and I was stuck in one place. I was practically zoned out for the entirety of dinner. I hoped no one would notice, but of course, I wouldn't be that lucky. Kyle, Taylor, and Perri were all shooting me concerned looks throughout dinner. The only person who actually knew what was going on was Kyle, but that didn't mean that the other two couldn't be concerned or care. I mean, I don't understand why Perri really cared; she barely knows me, and we're barely friends, if I can even call whatever this is friendship. She doesn't need to fill her brain space worrying about me and my fucked-up problems.

When we got back to the hotel at night, I just went straight to my room. I was just so tired. I didn't care about Chanukah; everyone would just have to understand. I had to just go to bed. Tomorrow would be a better day. It had to be. And I would feel better tomorrow.

Chapter Eight

W hen I left my room the next morning, my parents looked angry. My mom's face was bright red, and I knew I had messed up. I didn't want to say anything. I didn't want to start a fight. It wasn't necessary. Not today. Not right now.

I was expecting my parents to be angry. That was a given. After what I had pulled last night, they should have been angry. I gave them every reason to be angry. I was angry with myself. I couldn't believe what I had pulled either. However, I didn't want to talk about it. It was far too much for me to deal with right now. I'm supposed to be here and have fun on this trip, and I'm not. Well, I wouldn't say I'm not having fun on this trip; it's just that I'm not having as much fun as I should because my anxiety is holding me back and keeping me from doing what I would like to be doing. It's nothing against the wonderful friends I have gotten to spend time with on the trip. I love them to death. If anything, they are making this trip bearable. Without them beside me, I don't know if I'd be able to ski at all. I might as well just sit in the hotel room all day, curled up with a book in my lap at this state.

My mother glared at me as I began to make myself breakfast quietly. I knew she wanted to talk about the night before and about me skipping Chanukah. What did she want from me? Out of Evangeline and me, I was never her favorite. I was always trying to take care of everything so that her favorite daughter wasn't the one to disappoint her. I'm used to this look of disappointment on her face. This is normal for me.

"We need to talk about last night," she said when I sat down with my egg sandwich. "We'll let it slide this one time, but you can't keep missing out on Chanukah and lighting the candles with us every night. I don't care how tired you are, we are all lighting the candles together. Understood?"

I nodded. There was a small part of me that wanted to fight. A part of me that wanted to tell her that the only reason I skipped out on lighting the candles was because I had such a rough day, and my mental health has been so bad since losing Evangeline. I wanted to tell her that I couldn't even ski yesterday. That it took me all morning to be able to just ski down a run I had never thought twice about skiing down. A run that only gives me anxiety when it's so crowded with people who don't know what they're doing that I'm worried I might hit one of them. That's the only time I've ever worried about what skiing down that run might look like. Until yesterday, when I could barely make it three feet before stopping because the easiest run on the mountain was no longer the easiest. The easiest run on the mountain had become so hard and so overwhelming that I could barely move my body more than three feet before I'd feel as though I forgot how to breathe yet again. Until I would feel as though my legs and my brain had become disconnected, and I couldn't make sense of what was going on with my legs enough to guide myself down the run.

But I couldn't tell her any of that. I didn't need her to worry about my mental state because I couldn't ski down an easy run. I didn't want to get stuck in ski lessons with grown men who had never skied before because I couldn't push

myself down the easiest run. I didn't want to be a disappointment. I've always been the kid they didn't need to worry
about. I wasn't about to change that because I couldn't pull
myself together now.

So, I just nodded and focused on my breakfast. It wasn't
the best strategy, but it was the one that would help me the
most. I wasn't facing the truth, at least not in front of them.
They don't need to know how much I'm failing and how I'm
barely able to hold myself up long enough to make it through
the day. I may have lost my sister, but they lost their daughter.
They are hurting too. They don't need to deal with my pain
alongside theirs. They have enough going on anyway.

"I'm sorry," I whispered. My face felt warm as tears
sprung to my eyes. There was no use in trying to keep them
at bay. My mother's face softened as the first tear fell. For the
first time since Evangeline's death, I felt like she might actually take care of me instead of the other way around. "I just
miss her so much. Being here without her feels so wrong."

My mom came over and sat down next to me, wrapping
her arms around me. She didn't need to say anything in that
moment. She just held me in a way that made me feel so
loved and cared for.

We ate breakfast as a family in silence. It was weird (not
that we were eating in silence, more so that we were eating
together). I can't remember the last time that actually
happened. Things have gotten pretty weird since Evangeline
died, and honestly, I hadn't even noticed that we weren't
eating meals together, just the three of us, until we were faced
with that. It was the first breakfast we were actually having as
a family without Evangeline forcing us to have some kind of
conversation. Without her, we always fell into a comfortable
silence at the table. Now the lack of her presence was stark
and glowing. It was clear that we were missing something
very important. Someone very important.

I rushed to get ready and meet up with my friends. I just

needed to get out of that room. I couldn't bear to be in there any longer. I was itching to get onto the slopes, itching to feel closer to my sister. I just wanted to feel as though we were skiing together again. Maybe I would have to push myself farther than I thought I'd have to in order to feel close to her again. Sometimes these things just happen, I guess. I wasn't even sure if I was ready to push myself down runs I might not be ready for, but I was grasping at any little fragment of closeness to my sister again.

I rushed to the ski valet to pick up my skis. My boots were uncomfortable, as they had always been, but I didn't mind. I needed to get back onto those slopes. I also had this odd desire to spend time with Perri. She was so kind and sweet, and I just wanted to spend more time with her. It was becoming clear to me that she and Kyle had spent a lot of time together when they were growing up. She was practically the female version of him. She held the same kindness and love for me that he did. Except, she had known me for only a few days, and he had known me for years. I didn't even bat an eye at it though.

We all took the bubble up. I sat in the middle between Kyle and Perri, with Taylor on the other side of Kyle. The three of them were talking on our way up the lift, but honestly, I couldn't focus on it too much. I didn't really want to. I was scared that if I looked at Kyle, I would just start crying again, and that was the last thing I wanted to do. I just wanted to exist in my own little world without having to deal with the chaos of those around me.

Taylor and Kyle really wanted to go down Echo, so we split off from them, and Perri and I made our way down High Meadow. I was starting to get used to leading us down the run. It's not my favorite thing to do. I've always been a follower, but I know that Perri only wants to follow me down the run out of concern that I might have an issue and need her help. She was a ski instructor back home, after all. She was used to getting paid to deal with kids like me. This is her normal.

When we made it to the bottom of the run, I was feeling quite confident. It was as if we hadn't taken any steps backward since skiing down at the end of the day yesterday. I was ready to keep going onto something harder. We skied over to the Saddleback lift, and before we knew it, we were on our way up. That's one of my favorite parts of skiing in the morning. It always seems to feel as though there aren't as many people on the mountain.

"You know Kyle and I used to be really close when we were little," Perri said as we slowly made our way up the lift. "That was before he moved out to you, before middle school. He used to live right down the street from me. We hung out all the time. He was practically my brother."

"He never said anything about that, but he's always been more of the class clown. Especially in middle school. It took a few years before I was able to have a serious conversation with him."

"He really knows how to make anyone smile. I wasn't surprised when my parents finally decided to file for divorce. They've been fighting for years. I remember one time when I was about ten, it got so bad that my dad just left for a week. My mom was a complete wreck. I think we spent more time with Kyle and his parents than we did at our own home. I think my mom just really needed her big brother. I spent that week sleeping on the floor of Kyle's room. That whole week he refused to leave my side."

"He did the exact same thing when my sister died. At times, I felt like I had no privacy, but I wouldn't have changed a thing. Taylor just started getting super distant around then; I was lucky to just have someone by my side." We both sat in a comfortable silence for the rest of the lift ride up. Maybe spending this week with Perri wasn't going to be so bad after all.

We made our way back to the Red Pine base area, and I had some choices to make. I could take Perri down Kokopelli, but did I really want to? I mean, the run is nice and all, but I never know what's going to happen when I get on it. It is very steep and can be icy. There have been times I've skied down the run without a problem, but there have been other times where I have just had a serious issue and have had bad panic attacks on that very run. People like to go down that run when they shouldn't, so I've even gotten hit by snowboarders on the run before. We were both fine. Now it's just a funny story. I wish someone had a video of it. We could go down Chicane. I did want to stop at Tombstone for lunch since it is the best food on the mountain, but I wasn't sure if timing was on my side.

I decided Chicane would probably be a better idea. Depending on how long it would take us, we could probably do one or two more runs before lunch. Maybe we'd go over to Iron Mountain and take Copperhead before heading in for lunch. That would be really fun. Copperhead has always been one of my favorite runs, especially when the conditions are perfect. We might actually be able to get a table inside Tombstone since we are just the two of us. That would be so much nicer than having to eat outside in the cold.

I led Perri over to Chicane, and we began to head down it. I don't really like the beginning of the run because it's super flat and hard to get moving on. I normally have to skate for a good amount before I am able to start skiing down it.

Before we started to go down the run, Perri pulled me over to the side. "I'm sure you've been down this run hundreds of times, but I do want to put some little thoughts into your head to help with your skiing since yesterday. First, just focus on what's in front of you. There is so much going on while skiing each individual run. Just focus on the next few feet ahead of you and not the bottom of the run. Think of all the different parts of the run that might be good places to take a break. Those are your checkpoints. You can stop at each one. Also, I know you have taken lessons all your life and are used to having form grilled into you, but remember that you are here to have fun. Your form doesn't matter. As long as you are not in pain and having fun, that is all I care about right now."

Her smile was wide as I nodded. She was right. I could break this run up into three separate chunks in my head: before the bypass, the bypass, and after the bypass. The part after the bypass is my favorite, and I know that once I get there, I will be okay.

I was also planning on taking her down the Chicane Bypass. The bottom half of Chicane, before where it meets the bypass, can get steep and is a little difficult for me, and I prefer to go down the bypass. It is just easier for me to ski down.

I took the beginning of the run slow. I wasn't going to push myself. I wasn't sure I was really ready to do so. At least not yet. I just had to focus on the next few turns ahead of me. Since it was still pretty early, the run wasn't too crowded. I was able to stop focusing on everything that was right in front of me. The people in front of me just faded into part of the run, and before I knew it, I was at the bypass. Perri's advice had helped. When I stopped worrying about making it down the run, skiing became so much easier.

I led Perri down to the bypass, and then we began to go down my favorite part of the run. When we made it down to the bottom of the run, I was faced with more options. It was about 10:30, and I didn't want to sit down for lunch for at least an hour. I did jwant to have lunch early because the restaurants on the mountain start to get crowded at noon and 1:00. An earlier lunch is always better than a later one, in my opinion. I'd rather eat earlier than try and find a table when the restaurant is packed.

When we got into the Tombstone base area, Perri's eyes

went wide. The three lifts and wonderful barbecue restaurant were a surprising sight. I wasn't sure where to lead her next. It was the first time I didn't have an instructor with me telling me where to go and what runs to go down. It was all up to me. It was my choice, and a choice that I had to make.

I decided that we had just enough time to head over to take my sister's favorite run before lunch. Perri and I made our way over to my favorite two-way lift, Timberline. The line wasn't long at all, and we were able to get a chair to ourselves. However, we had to deal with my least favorite part of the lift: climbing up to the loading spot. On the Tombstone side of the lift, it is always harder to get to the loading spot, and if you are not good at climbing up something on skis, good luck. For the duration of the ride, we waved, smiled, and made faces at anyone we saw coming from the opposite direction. People had all sorts of things to say to us, and we couldn't help but laugh at the absurdity of some of what was said.

We then got off Timberline and made our way toward the Iron Mountain lift. The orange chairs were a stark contrast from the white snow. The line for the lift was nonexistent, so we made our way up to the chair and then up the lift. I was excited to ski down Copperhead.

The first time I skied down Copperhead, I saw the trees in the middle of the run and the only thing I could think was "I'm going to hit a tree." I couldn't get that out of my head. Somehow, I didn't end up hitting a tree and have loved the run ever since. It also helps that it was Evangeline's favorite run. She was with me the first time I went on the run. She led, of course, and even though the run was a bit icy, it was some of the most fun we've had.

As I skied down the run, I felt so confident that it was almost magical. I felt like I knew what I was doing, where I was going, when I didn't really have a clue at all. Except, I did. I had done this run a million times; the only thing that ever changed was the people all around. Even the trees looked just like they did the last time we were here. It was a confidence I hadn't been expecting. It was so empowering to be able to ski down the run with such a force. The run was practically empty, and that only increased the fun. It was everything I had wanted and more.

Skiing the run I loved so much felt like a giant hug. The run itself was, in a way, comforting. It made me think of my sister. It reminded me of all the times she would take me down the run after ski school. Our parents would have her meet up with me when I would finish up, and she would convince me that we had to do a run together before heading in to our parents. So, she would always race me all the way to Timberline. I think that was just her way of getting me to ski as fast as I possibly could. It was worth it though; we would only be out for an extra half hour or so. Although, our parents never really seemed to notice or care.

But Evangeline would always race me down runs in an attempt to get me to ski faster. It was her way of trying to teach me to make fewer turns. She would rarely pass me during the races, but she would ski close behind me screaming, "faster! Ski faster Aubrey! I'm going to beat you if you don't speed up!" I would always think of her behind me and whatever anxiety might have been there before just seemed to melt away.

Going down the run, it felt like she was right beside me the whole time. It was like we were actually skiing together again. For the first time in months, I was able to feel her presence so strongly, stronger than I had in the past few months. It was something I didn't know I needed, but feeling her so near in that moment caused a sense of calm to wash over me. I took each turn with the relaxed confidence I had been struggling to find. I was in my element and in the best mental space I had been in since her death. Yet, she was with me the whole time.

When Perri and I made it to the bottom of the run, it was time to go grab some food. I was very hungry at that point and was in need of my favorite pulled pork sandwich from the Tombstone Grill.

We popped our skis off and found a table to put our stuff down at before heading inside to order. We both ordered our food at the window on the side of the building and received our buzzers before heading back to the table with our drinks to eagerly wait for our food.

We had arrived at the restaurant a bit later than we had planned, so we didn't end up getting a table inside, but there were very few occupied tables outside.

It was the first time that Perri and I were really alone, just the two of us. I didn't really know how to act or what to do with myself. I wanted to start a conversation, but I really didn't know anything about the girl in front of me to have any idea of what to say to her. I wished I had a better idea of what to say or how to talk to someone that wasn't Taylor or Kyle, but one on one with her, I was at a total loss. I felt like I was the weirdo who googles "how to talk to another person" or "how to make friends" because I was completely incapable.

I was pretty much saved by my buzzer going off. I jumped up and made my way to the side door for my wonderful sandwich. I was so excited to sink my teeth into the bread, meat, and the cornbread with honey butter that was sitting on the side of my tray. Perri's buzzer went off not too long after mine, and she popped up just as quickly and ran to grab her food. She had ordered the brisket platter. Her face lit up with pure bliss when she took her very first bite, and she looked so cute that I wished I could have taken a picture. Skiing with her was a total dream, and now that I wasn't so completely focused on my sister, I realized we might have a bigger problem. I might have a bit of a crush.

Chapter Nine

After we finished eating, we got up, put all the gear we had taken off back on, and then got our skis back on. We made our way over to Timberline. I wanted to take Copperhead again, and then I had some ideas for some other runs we could take. I thought it would just be a lot of fun. Perri didn't know much about the mountain to know what runs there were, so I was able to pick the runs I like and the runs I think are nice, fun, and chill. However, I didn't want to be too adventurous. This was only our second day skiing. I didn't want to push myself too far. Even though I feel as though I'm over whatever was haunting me yesterday, there is still a small fear in the back of my mind that I might not be as capable as I thought I was. Maybe I can't do as much as I thought I could. Maybe I'll never be able to ski in the way that I used to. What if I'm never the same again?

We skied Copperhead again, and it was nice seeing Perri navigate the run differently after having been down it once before. Since I was pretty confident in my skiing down the run, I asked if she would take a turn leading us down the run. I could see she was hesitant. If I was skiing with me, I'd be hesitant too. But I just want her to have fun too. I knew she felt the same way my friends had felt for years. The second she leads us down the run and begins to fully enjoy it for herself, I will have a panic attack and need her to come and help me get down the run.

After going down that run, we got back on the Iron Mountain lift, and I decided to take her to some of my other favorite pockets on the mountain. My confidence was clearly up since we had skied yesterday, and that opened up so many other fun runs for us to ski down. With my confidence back up to where it had been every year previous, we had so many more opportunities to ski down all of my favorite runs.

Copperhead a second time was nice and easy. I love the landscape of the run. Since the first time I had been down the run, I realized that I had gotten so much better at not hitting trees and just skiing freely, knowing that the trees can stay there and I can make my way around them without having to worry about them being in my way.

"You mentioned earlier that some of your favorite runs are over here," Perri said with a smile on her face as we made our way over to the Iron Mountain lift for the fifth time that day.

I smiled. I was shocked that she had been paying so much attention to the runs I had claimed to love. "Yeah, maybe we should switch things up this time and I can take you over to my favorite run," I replied with a smile. I so badly wanted to get her over to Harmony. It was probably my favorite run on the entire mountain. It was a run that I always felt so confident on that it was startling.

"I'll follow your lead; you decide where to take me." She smiled at me, and it was comforting. Just looking at her in that moment, I wanted to get to know everything about her. I wanted to know every facet of her personality. I wanted to know who she was on the inside and outside. I wanted to know who she was with her friends versus who she was with her family. I wanted her all to myself. I wanted her alone, even though it felt as though we would never be truly alone together.

I followed the signs to the Dreamcatcher lift. The runs were nice and calm, and we just ended up having a nice day where there weren't a lot of people around to fill the run and make me just slightly more anxious. There was this one pitch through the trees that Perri really wanted to ski down. It wasn't more than a couple of feet, but it was pretty steep. Perri lit up when she did it and was begging me to join her down the little pitch. It wasn't anything special from where we were, and I figured it couldn't hurt. But I don't love going fast. I always want to be in control, and skiing fast always makes me feel as though I'm out of control. But with the right mindset, I could ski anything. I've learned that from years of skiing. I have the abilities to ski whatever I want. I just have to get past the anxiety that is holding me back from skiing the runs I want to.

I took a deep breath, and with Perri cheering me on from the bottom of the run, I finally felt I had the small amount of confidence necessary to make it down that small pitch. I went for it, and the speed shocked me at first. I felt for a second that I was out of control, but when I stopped next to Perri and my hockey stop sprayed her with snow, I couldn't have been happier. I had found control within the speed I thought I would never be able to control. I could do it. Whatever I wanted to do. If I set my mind to it, I could do it.

We then made our way over to the Dreamcatcher lift and got on. That lift was even emptier than Iron Mountain was. If I thought that lift was empty, this lift had so few people on it that it shouldn't have even been running. We got off the lift, and I brought Perri to one of my other favorite runs, Panorama. It's a nice, calm run. And we had perfect timing. With it being so close to lunchtime, all the people near that run were going to the restaurant Cloud Dine, which was right at the top of the lift. Anyone on the nearby lifts was going to get lunch, and that left us with a pretty chill and open space to be able to ski on.

We made our way to the bottom of the run, and then I took Perri down my other favorite run, Harmony. Harmony is the one run that I am able to just ski freely down. As soon as I get on the run, I just point my skis downhill and am just able to go. I fly down the run as freely as possible. It always feels so nice to be able to just point my skis down and let them carry me.

When we made it to the bottom of Harmony, we finally got on the Tombstone lift. We had enough time for a few more runs before we would have to go in for the day. So, we took Red Pine Road back to the Red Pine base area. From there, we headed back down to Chicane. Skiing down Chicane at the end of the day is always so nice for some reason. Even though I generally hate the conditions of the run at the end of the day, there is something special about skiing down it at my own pace. It might have something to do with the fact that I used to ski down it at the end of the day with Evangeline sometimes, but it felt way more freeing when it's one of the last runs than when it is during the day.

Yet, skiing in general without an instructor feels more freeing. It has been so nice to be able to just pick the run you want to go down or where you want to eat (and at least for me, with Perri who doesn't know anything about the mountain we are on) without having to really check with a whole group of people. Or, in my case, there have been so many times I've had to go down a run that I was just not comfortable going down, and since I was with a group where other people wanted to go down the run, I didn't have much of a choice as to whether I wanted to go down it or not.

When we got to the Tombstone base area, I led Perri to the Over and Out lift. We would be taking one more run before heading back to the hotel.

The line at the lift wasn't too large when we got there. It

was at the point in the day where most people had already gone in, and we were among the stragglers who were going in as the mountain was closing. It was much better than the days when the lift gets really packed and the line to ski down at the end of the day seems to last forever.

We took our time skiing down to really feel the snow under our skis, or at least so I could feel it the best that I could. I wanted and needed to just be in the moment. As I was heading back to the hotel and would be off the mountain momentarily, my brain was buzzing with the million different things I needed to do and know regarding my day and what I was doing. But I didn't want to pull my focus from skiing. I wanted to be focused on the skiing and feel the wind in my face and the warmth of my gloves. I wanted to stay present. I needed to stay present.

I walked through the ski beach area and checked my skis into the valet, then made my way toward the hotel. I got my room key ready so that I would be able to get into the room myself.

Kyle was sitting on the couch watching TV when I walked into the condo. It wasn't unusual for Taylor or Kyle to come over after we were all done skiing. We would always spend nights playing card games, video games, or just hanging out when we weren't on the mountain, so this wasn't much of a shock for me.

"You really went all day," he said without turning from the TV. "How was skiing with Perri?"

"She's really fun to ski with," I replied as I began to take off any gear that needed to be hung up out here (jacket, helmet, gloves, etc.), facing away from him as I began to blush.

"That's it? That's all I'm going to get? She's fun? You've got to have more to say than that!" I rolled my eyes at his comment. He was starting to sound like a parent. What I wanted to say was that I was actually having an amazing time and Perri's really pretty, and I think I have a little crush on her, but how do I say that to her cousin? And I've only known her for two days. A pretty girl was nice to me and now I have a crush? That seems like a bit much.

"What else do you want me to say?" I was starting to get annoyed. I just wanted to take a shower. "I had fun, and the skiing was nice, but it was just weird today." I took my boots off and began to head up the stairs.

"Perri's really cool. You just need to get to know her better. Spending more time with her will help. All friendships start out awkward anyway. You can't get past awkward without talking to her though. So tomorrow, I need you to start a conversation with her that is about anything other than skiing." I just sighed and made my way over to my room. Who was Kyle to be telling me how I need to make friends and how I should be doing just that?

When I got up to my room, I went over to the closet where my casual clothes were and picked out an outfit to wear for dinner. We would be going into town and had a reservation at one of my favorite restaurants. I couldn't wait to go.

I then got in the shower, where I could finally relax for the first time all day. I let the warm water run down my back as I fell into my own little world inside my head. I let my thoughts consume me, but not in an anxiety-provoking way, in a calming and caring kind of way.

Once I was out of the shower, I began to get ready for dinner. I changed into my casual clothes and then from there, threw my hair up in a towel so it wouldn't soak the back of my shirt. I went back to my room and just moved around for a little bit, tidying things up and making the room look nice, before I took the towel down and hung it up. I then did my makeup and blew out my hair for dinner.

I stared out the window for most of the drive into town. I wanted to take in the sights. I loved getting to see everything just like I had with my sister nearly two years prior. It was sad to see how much had changed in the past year. Change is normally such a good thing, or at least it's supposed to be, but now all of this change just reminds me of what Evangeline will never get to see.

She used to hate the way I would stare out the window in a trance-like state. I don't blame her; if I was trying to hang out with me, I would hate that I do it too. But without her beside me to bug me about it, I didn't even notice that I began to do it. It was just second nature to me. No one bothered me. I'm sure Kyle didn't want to talk to me after my outburst when I got back to the hotel room anyway.

As the bus drove along, we passed a mountain that was open for night skiing. We could see the skiers coming down the lit trails, and I wished that I could do that. It had always been a dream of mine. One day, I would come here and ski that mountain at night. Evangeline and I always wanted to do that together. She used to talk about how we were going to do it when we were both eighteen and our parents would let us go out at night together. I don't know if I want to do it anymore. It doesn't feel right to want to do it without her.

When the bus came to a stop in town, everyone rushed to jump up and run off. I, however, was in no rush to get off and understood that my time would come, so I let all of the eager people run past me. Then, I got off with the rest of the people who didn't think it was that big of a deal to be running off the bus.

We went to the Wasatch Brewery. I was honestly pretty excited to be eating at the brewery. It had been one of my favorite restaurants for a few years when I was little, and it has been comforting in the past few years.

We had to wait for a table for no longer than fifteen minutes. We were very lucky. I'm sure there were other groups of people from our school that went to restaurants that had way longer wait times.

We sat down at the table and all went silent as we looked

over the menu and decided what we would be ordering. I was really just looking over the menu briefly, but I had a pretty good idea of what I would be getting. I just wanted to see if there was anything new on the menu since I was last here.

However, I found that nothing really changed and I was still planning on getting the loaded mac and cheese. The dish was just always so good and I couldn't wait for it. They used to have a tuna tartar on their menu and it was one of my favorite dishes. I don't miss it all that much though, I can get tuna tartar at almost every restaurant we go to. It's nice to have some diversity in what I'm eating.

We ordered our food, and then all we had to do was wait. We chatted for a little bit, but when the food arrived, we all just ate in silence.

After dinner, we decided to just hang out around Main Street and grab some dessert during the hour we had before we would have to get back on the bus to head back to the hotel for the night.

When we got back to the hotel, everyone gathered in our room to light the candles and do Chanukah. We passed around gifts as we watched the warm glow of the candles. When I went into my suitcase to grab some gifts for my friends, I was shocked to find Evangeline's gift sitting in the bag with the rest of them. My mom said she had packed all of my wrapped gifts, and I guess neither one of us realized that this gift wasn't one for anyone in this room. I had bought Evangeline a little keychain a few months before she passed, right after her birthday. It feels silly now, looking at the little wrapped keychain. It had an elephant skiing on it. It was something I just knew she was going to love. It was too late to be her birthday present, so I would just have to wait until Chanukah. I wrapped it and hid it. I had practically forgotten about it. I guess I had even forgotten where I hid it because I hid all of my other Chanukah gifts in the same place.

I heard a knock on my door and was shocked to see it was Perri standing in the doorway. "Everyone's opening gifts and Kyle sent me to check on you. He's wondering what's been taking so long."

"It's nothing," I said, standing up and grabbing my bag of second and third-night gifts for my friends and family. I didn't even realize I was holding the keychain in my hand. I had torn the wrapping paper, and it looked like a sad excuse for a wrapped gift. I looked down at it and then shoved it into my pocket.

"Doesn't look like nothing." She smirked at me. I wanted to shake her off. I wanted to push her away, but at the same time, I just wanted her to hold me and comfort me as I get through this rough time.

"It was supposed to be a gift for my sister," I pulled the keychain out of my pocket and fully unwrapped it. "I've had it for like eight months. I found it a few months after her birthday, right before she, you know, and I thought she'd love it but since it was so far from her birthday, I figured it would be best if I just waited until Chanukah. That seemed like the next logical time to give her a gift. It's not that big of a deal though. It's just a keychain. You can have it if you want. I forgot I even had it." I felt tears begin to well up, and the last thing I wanted to do was cry again.

Perri got really close to me and put her hand over mine, causing me to shut up, and I felt goosebumps spring up all over my arms. I was lucky I was wearing a long-sleeved shirt so she didn't see me getting all flustered at her simple gesture. "It's not nothing." She said in a low whisper. Her face was mere inches from mine. I had only known her for a few days, yet I hoped that what I wanted to happen was about to happen. I wanted her to kiss me in that moment. I wanted to be hers.

And before I could even process it, that's exactly what happened. Her soft lips were on mine. Just for a brief moment. I didn't even know how to react to it, if I'm being honest. When she pulled away, her face was as red as I felt mine was.

"Thank you," was all I could manage. Kyle might have been right about me needing to get to know her, but it wasn't in the way that he had intended. He didn't realize that she already knew so much about me. I had given her everything she might have needed. She had access to every facet of my being. She already knew my anxiety just as my friends do, if not better. She may even know it in the way that my sister used to.

She smiled back at me and grabbed my bag of gifts for that night and the night prior, and we walked into the living room where our families were waiting for us together.

I went to bed that night with this warm feeling that reminded me of my sister and the life she once lived.

Chapter Ten

I woke up to a morning that was just like the day before. I woke up to my alarm blaring, then ate breakfast, had coffee, and got ready for the day. Everything was down to routine. I was practically flying ahead on autopilot. I really didn't even have to think about anything I was doing for the majority of the beginning of my morning. Even getting on the bubble seemed mundane and routine. And it was only day three. However, as we stood in line to get on the lift, I couldn't help but be reminded of this one time I had been skiing with my sister.

We were around thirteen to fifteen at the time. It was before my parents made sure that I was in lessons, and Evangeline and I were skiing together. It was our lucky day; we would be skiing just us two. It was the two of us with the whole mountain at our fingertips. Anything could and would happen.

The day was filled with a bunch of little moments, but my favorite moment from that day happened at the Orange Bubble. We had gotten in line, and anyone would have thought it was just a normal day, and I honestly thought it was too. It had been a normal ski day until we got on that line. Well, it was more like when we got up to the chair. Evangeline and I were deep in conversation—I don't remember what it was about—but the chair was coming around and the conversation kept going and neither one of us turned around or looked when the chair came up behind us and knocked both of us on our asses and the lift had to be stopped. We didn't get hurt and we both thought it was so funny both in the moment and after the fact.

So now, every time I go to get on the bubble, I can't help but think of that moment and think of all the fun Evangeline and I would have together on our ski trips. I will never forget how happy she would be when skiing and when we were in Utah. At home, she would almost be a shell of the person I saw in Utah. I would occasionally be able to see glimpses of the girl that I knew to be my sister. I could always pull that girl out of her, no matter the circumstances.

We got on the lift and headed up for the day, and the excitement of another ski day bubbled inside of me. The confidence I had gained yesterday propelled me down our first run, making some of the most beautiful turns I have ever made. Yet, being with Perri caused anxiety to thrum through my veins. How was I supposed to just act like everything was normal after she kissed me last night? How could anyone?

We skied down High Meadow, and then Perri and I made our way to the Saddleback lift. I figured it would be a nice start to the morning for us to go down the same run we had started with the day before. I might even want to take my favorite tree path through Snow Dancer, Flying Salmon. It's a fun run once you get into it, but there is a bit of it that is uphill, which makes it somewhat frustrating. Once I'm past that part, though, the run is so much fun.

As soon as we got on the Saddleback lift, Perri began to get really excited. She had really enjoyed the run the day before and couldn't wait to do it again. Assuming we'd be going down the same run as the day before, she asked if she could lead me down it. I was all for that. She was so cute when she got excited. The way her face lit up and her eyes went wide as I suggested Saddleback was priceless.

When we got off the lift, she took off down the mountain. She skied fast and beautifully. Her form was beautiful. It was what many of my previous instructors had referred to as a "mom skier" with her narrow stance and gorgeous turns. I have always strived to have that kind of form. I always think it looks really good and have always wanted to be able to do it myself, but I tend to have a very wide stance.

I was really enjoying watching Perri ski. It was to the point where I was so distracted by watching her that I wasn't paying attention to anything else. My only focus was on her. It was like the rest of the world disappeared. Nothing else mattered except watching Perri ski, and with my eyesight (even with my contacts in), I found that the closer I was, the better I could see her skiing.

When she veered onto Flying Salmon, I didn't even really realize that was where we were. I had mentioned wanting to go on it when we were on the lift, but I didn't think she was really paying attention to it. I was so engulfed in my tunnel where all I could see was her. Maybe that wasn't the safest thing because I should have been paying attention to everything around me, but it is what it is, I guess. I didn't run into anyone, so I would consider that to be a win.

When we got to the bottom of the run, I figured we'd do something a little different and new. I decided to brave the one run that I both love and hate: Kokopelli.

The run has always been one that I enjoy, but there are times when I go to get on the run and I just start panicking because it's steep, icy, and too much for me to handle. But I always have enjoyed the run because it gets me to one of my favorite tree runs on the mountain, Hurricane Alley. The run can be easily missed. There isn't a sign pointing the run out, so I always feel like it's my little secret.

The first time I go down Hurricane Alley each year, I always have trouble with it. I need to take it slow to make sure I don't have an issue, but once I know what has changed since the previous year, I can fly down it no problem. It's one of the most fun runs on the mountain. If only I didn't need to take Kokopelli to get to it. That run is an absolute nightmare.

We got in line for Saddleback for the second time that day, and it took about fifteen minutes before we were on a chair. We were on our way up. I wanted to talk to Perri about last night and figure out where we stood now, but there was another couple on the chair with us, and they were very quiet. I didn't want to bother them with our random conversation, so I just kept to myself. I'll do it later.

We got off the lift, and I began to get incredibly anxious. As soon as I could see Kokopelli, I felt this overwhelming rush of anxiety in anticipation of what was going to happen. I could get on the run, and everything would be fine, and I would be able to get down it fine and not have a problem. But I also could get on the run and find myself side slipping down the left side of the run slowly and anxiously because it's steep, kind of scary, and icy.

But I wouldn't know if I didn't go down it, would I?

I led Perri onto the run and began to take my first few routine turns. Things felt pretty okay, so I was able to keep on going and making small turns. It was one after the other. If I could just focus on the turn in front of me and not the whole run, then I could just get down the run. I stuck to the side I was more comfortable on. It has always seemed to me that people tend to veer to the other side of the run, which can make this side less icy. At least that's what I tell myself to convince myself to keep skiing down it.

Somehow, I was able to do it. Maybe it was because the run wasn't all that icy, or maybe it was because I had been down the run so many times, I knew what was coming so I was able to just focus on the turn right in front of me. But whatever it was, it got me to the end of the steep part in the run without having much of a problem.

We then got to the split in the runs by the sign, and I began to lead Perri down Hurricane Alley. I was nervous. Hurricane Alley was a run I felt I could never trust. Every year, it looks different. It's on the map, but since there's no sign for it, a fallen tree might just become part of the run for the next year or so. Once it gets covered in snow, that's it. It's a new bump on the run. We went past the sign to a run that wasn't labeled.

I hadn't been down the run in so long that I was nervous going down it. The interesting thing about tree runs is that even if you've been on it before, it probably won't be the same a year later. Trees fall and change, and that's just nature. But if a tree falls and then snow covers it, it can create a new path through the run.

I cautiously and carefully made turns throughout the different areas of the run. I made sure to keep looking ahead of me and acknowledge every tree, branch, and twig scattered throughout the run.

I made it to the bottom of the run safely, as I had hoped. Neither one of us fell. Hurricane Alley is a run that can be lots of fun, but I've been with groups where people just can't stop falling. There was even one time that I had an issue on the run. I was very anxious and was skiing in a wedge. I got to one of the really narrow paths between two trees and somehow, I managed to be sideways. The path I was supposed to be skiing on was curved under my skis while my skis rested on the banks of snow on either side of the path. It took me nearly fifteen minutes to get my skis facing the correct way to be able to ski down the run. I was so stuck because there were trees on either side of me and the path was very narrow.

Once we got down to the base area after the run, we headed over to Chicane and the Chicane Bypass to head in for lunch. We got to lunch early enough where we could easily grab a table inside. We took off our gear, left it at the table, and then went up to the front to order our food. We then went back to the table to wait for our buzzers to go off.

"That run was really fun!" Perri said, as soon as we sat down with our food, nearly beaming at me. "How did you find out about it? I would have never realized there was a run there."

I smiled and tried not to blush. Why was I blushing? "I had an instructor who showed me it a few years ago. He took us down it almost every day. The entire group I skied with really loved it. I even introduced my family to it.

"You seem to take lessons a lot. It's nice, but you're old enough now to not have to take lessons anymore. Normally, people our age who have been skiing for as long as you have grown out of lessons by now. Why haven't you?" Perri seemed more concerned than interrogative, and I had to honor that. Her perspective as a ski instructor, being on the other side of it, was wild.

"Well, most people, and by most people I mean my parents and as you've seen now my friends, haven't wanted to deal with my anxiety. I know I can ski what Taylor and Kyle ski; I've been told I should be able to for years, but I tend to just get in my head about it. It's caused us some serious issues in the past and my family just deemed it safer for me. It's not meant to hurt me. That I know."

She smiled kindly. "You don't need an instructor to keep you safe. You need someone who is willing to compromise on what runs you go down. Luckily, you have me and I have no idea where anything is on this mountain. I need you as my guide. I'd probably get lost otherwise."

I couldn't help but laugh at the image of Perri getting lost on the mountain. "This is the first year in a while that I haven't gotten to ski with my sister. She's normally the only person in a group who will put up with my nonsense."

"Well, I wouldn't call it nonsense. I find it quite endearing." There I went blushing again.

"Well, I'm glad someone feels that way. I would never describe a panic attack as endearing. But if you enjoy it, maybe I'll do it more. If I could control that." I whispered the last part, hoping she wouldn't hear, but the look on her face said otherwise.

"That's not what I meant." She smirked, and I was brought back to kissing her last night. I wanted to do it again. I wanted to do it right now, but I didn't want to push her boundaries.

My eyes drifted to her lips. They were full and pink, and they looked so soft. I reached for my glass across the table and brushed my hand against hers (maybe purposefully; I will not admit to that). Our eyes met for a second, and I wanted to go back to last night for a minute. I hoped she felt the same way.

After skiing down Copperhead a couple of times, Perri and I decided to go get some hot chocolate. I thought it would be best if we headed over to the Red Pine Lodge to get some.We got back on the Timberline lift to head back over to the Tombstone base area. The lift was always a fun one. With people going both ways, it is always really fun and funny.

We then headed to the line for the Tombstone lift. The six-seater lift is always crowded, so it would take a little bit for us to get up to the chair itself. We were lucky; being a small group of two, we were able to fill in space that people needed filled to get a full chair up to the top.

We spent about twenty minutes in line before getting on the lift and heading up. The lift ride was relatively quiet for us. Neither one of us was really interested in talking with the other four people on the chair with us. It didn't help that we were on a chair with part of a ski school group. It was a small group of boys who were all kind of rowdy and loud, and it would have been weird for Perri and me to be having a conversation. And if I was going to talk to her about anything, it was going to be about last night. There was no way I was going to be able to talk to her about that in public. Private conversations shouldn't happen in public situations. Especially when it's on a ski lift with four pre-pubescent boys.

We got off the lift and headed to the right, which was the easiest way down, and we began to ski down a run called Red Pine Road. It would be taking us down to the Red Pine base area. It was the easiest run to get us there, and honestly, one of my favorites. It hasn't always been one that I've loved, but I have found in more recent years that the run is actually really beautiful, and I've grown to love it and enjoy the view, even though it can get very icy throughout the day as more and more people ski down it.

As we got to the bottom of the run, we saw this kid with a ski school group who was wearing a green helmet. He was skiing without poles and looked like he was about to lose control any second and crash. When he stopped with his group and they were all talking, he just took his skis off and just sat down. What a sight. Perri and I looked at each other and just started laughing. It was so nice and made me feel like we could actually be friends.

We headed inside and grabbed a table before grabbing a cup of hot chocolate and then making our way back. We sat there for a minute, just drinking our hot chocolate in silence. I just let the warmth run through my body and warm me up.

"So, what's your favorite run on the mountain?" Perri asked after a few minutes of us just sitting in silence.

"I think it changes every trip," I spoke. "I can find a run one year that I fall in love with but then the next year or next trip I feel a special connection to another run and then begin to fall in love with it."

"That's kind of cool! What run might be your favorite this trip?"

"I think it might be Copperhead. I've been really drawn to

it this trip. It was my sister's favorite run so that might have something to do with that."

Our conversation moved comfortably from there onto other random topics, as conversations do, before it was time for us to ski down for the day. We made our way to our skis and put them back on. Then, we made our way over to Chicane. We skied down the nice, long run and then took the Over and Out lift before deciding to ski down for the day.

There was this one time when we were little, Evangeline and I. Well, I guess we weren't that little. I was twelve, and she was ten. We were on our annual ski trip, and my parents had granted us the privilege to ski on our own. We were without them and without an instructor. We thought we were the coolest people on the mountain that day. We were playing around on an empty blue run, and she had her GoPro on. I decided to show her how I ski backward down a run (which is something that terrifies me), and I did it on a steeper part of a run. The fall I took was like one straight out of a cartoon. I tumbled down the run. When I stopped rolling down the mountain, she hockey stopped, spraying me with snow, and was holding all of my skis and poles and other things that I had lost in the fall. Of course, the whole thing was caught on video. We thought it was the funniest thing, but our parents weren't all that happy about it. We thought they would find it just as hilarious as we did, but we were back in lessons the next day and weren't allowed to go off on our own for a few years after that. But ever since my anxiety got worse, she always made sure to get one day with me where we would go off just the two of us. I wish she was still here to ski with.

Chapter Eleven

We got back to the hotel after skiing and went our separate ways. I needed to shower and get the day off me. Skiing had been fun, but I was far too sweaty.

I walked into the room and sat down to pull my boots off. I couldn't wait to have them off my feet. My shin had been rubbing up against the boot the whole day, as it probably should, and even though they weren't even close to bruised, they were red and irritated.

I'll never get over the feeling of taking off ski boots. I've always thought that the pain I was experiencing came from wearing my boots wrong. I've always figured they were probably too loose, but I couldn't make them tighter if I tried. I still need help getting them as tight as they are normally. But once I'm skiing, I always feel like I'm slightly bouncing in my boots as I go down bumpier runs, and it's always made me question if that is why my shins hurt so much when I take off my boots.

I mean, ski boots are never that comfortable. I don't know who invented them, but I wish they had invented something a little more comfortable. Maybe something that I could walk up and down stairs in at a normal pace rather than a very slow one. I wish ski boots were more like snowboarding boots. Every year, I see people walking around in them and wish my boots could be nearly as comfortable as theirs look. Although, I've never actually tried on their boots, so I wouldn't know. Snowboarders do scare me sometimes. But that's a personal thing I need to get over. They have a harder time when they get onto the slopes since they only have one thick board instead of the two thin skis strapped to each of my feet.

I got in the shower and relaxed as the warm water hit my skin. Any ounce of stress that I was holding in my body melted away with the water. I was finally able to relax and breathe.

As I stood in the shower, shampoo running down my hair and back, I just wanted to cry. The calm that I felt in that moment was just so overwhelming. How could I feel so calm and okay? The only person who ever made me feel this relaxed was my sister, and she is no longer here to bring that feeling back to me. How dare I feel so calm. How dare I even take a second and feel normal again, even if it's just in the shower when no one is watching. When I'm in public, I always feel like I need to act as though I feel okay and act as though everything is okay, even though I feel like I'm falling apart. And sometimes, I have these moments where life begins to feel normal again. Where I start to feel like I did in the time before Evangeline's death. But every time I catch myself, I feel guilty. I shouldn't be allowed to be happy without her. I shouldn't be allowed to relax without her. This shouldn't be allowed.

But then I think about the moment Perri kissed me. It was such a sweet moment, a moment where I felt even happier than I had when I was with Evangeline. Now that I really have time to go over the events in my head, to really think about how it all went down, I can't go tell Evangeline about it. Evangeline wasn't sitting in the hotel room when I got back, like she normally would be if we weren't skiing together. I'll never get the chance to go to her and scream all giddy and excited about what this relationship with Perri might be turning into. She'll never hear about any of my future relationships, romantic or platonic. I'll never get to rant to her about another bad test grade, I'll never get to hear about her first prom, or watch her get ready for her first prom. I'll never get to take a picture with her before my senior prom. I'll never get to celebrate my graduation with her. I'll never know where she would have gone to college.

Before I knew it, I was sitting on the floor of the shower in a puddle of tears. I know I should want to be happy and want to find a way to move on while still honoring her memory, but that sounds like an oxymoron. How can I move on and grow from this when I know I'm inherently leaving her behind? I'm supposed to just move forward with my life, and she doesn't get to come along with me. I don't get to have her by my side for whatever is to come. I don't get to support her in whatever the future would have held.

And here I am on the first vacation without her, having fun. No, I'm not just having fun, I'm having more fun than I've had in a very long time. More fun than I've allowed myself to have since Evangeline's death.

"But is that even the right thing to be doing or feeling? I mean, I know there's no right way to heal from this; everyone grieves in their own way. Yet, maybe I haven't considered what Evangeline wanted for our lives. Thinking about it makes her taking her own life feel so selfish, and then I wonder if I'm a bad sister for not catching it soon enough. Clearly, I was doing something wrong to let that happen to her. Clearly, I let her down. And I let my family down in the process. It's like the only thing I'm good at is letting people down, and that unfortunately ended in the loss of my sister."

However, when Perri kissed me, however short it was, I felt all that doubt, worry, and pain melt away, and I felt like myself again. I was finally myself again. Whatever that means. I was just starting to come to terms with the fact that maybe this was going to be my new normal. Maybe I was just going to live in a state of depression, not allowing myself to enjoy any moment because I know she'll never get to experience it. She'll never get the chance.

I stepped out of the shower and dried myself off before putting on the clothes I had grabbed for myself. Dinner tonight was going to be pretty low-key, and we were really just planning to walk around town for a bit. Nothing too exciting. I threw my hair up in a towel and walked out of the bathroom, letting the cold air hit my face. Maybe it will calm down some of the redness from all of the crying. I thought about putting on makeup. Nothing would cover up how I'm feeling like putting on makeup and acting like everything is perfect. But that would just be a lie. I'd have to dry my hair before we leave only because it is far too cold outside for me to go out with wet hair. I wouldn't want my hair to freeze. Not that I think my hair would be that wet by the time we would be leaving for dinner, but unfortunately, hair icicles are a real thing and something I would like to avoid if I can.

Exhaustion weighed me down, and I just wanted to crawl into bed and sleep for a year. I wanted to hide away and not have to go into town. I'd like to not even leave the room if I could. I'd just like to stay here and pretend the rest of the world doesn't exist for just a few minutes. I just want to be alone.

Maybe being alone isn't the best idea, but I'm not sure I

have the energy to deal with other people no matter how wonderful they are.

We met up with the rest of our large group in the hotel lobby as we waited for the shuttle to come pick us up to take us into town. Taylor, Kyle, and Perri were already huddled together in the midst of what looked like a very animated conversation. Though everything in me was screaming not to engage and to stay in my misery, I could only hope, and on some level, I knew that my friends would be able to meet me where I'm at regardless. It would be a more chill night. Not like there's much of a difference walking around town without much of an idea as to where we're going to be eating, but one involves going out farther. While that might not seem like a big difference, it's just longer I have to spend out with the rest of the group.

"Aubrey! Input. Now." Kyle called out the second he saw me, pulling me into the group and immediately engaging me in conversation. "Taylor and Perri both think this t-shirt is ridiculous, but I think it's a serve. What do you think?"

Kyle takes off his jacket to reveal a t-shirt underneath that says "I know I ski like an old man try to keep up!"

"Kyle, that shirt is awful! There's no way you're actually going to be wearing that out!" I laughed. "There's no way you're actually planning on wearing that!"

A serious look came across Kyle's face, and he almost looked offended for a second. "Of course, I was planning on wearing this! Do you really think I bought it to not wear it?"

"I really think you should go and cover it up!" Perri said, laughing so hard she was nearly in tears. "You can't seriously be considering wearing that, can you?"

"We're about to leave, I wasn't planning on changing."

"Kyle, you can't be serious," Taylor interjected. "You look insane."

"Come on, it's just a t-shirt! It really can't be that bad!"

"Oh, but it can!" Taylor and Perri said at the same time

before falling into a fit of giggles. I looked at my friends laughing at the absurdity of a shirt and couldn't help but feel the sadness creeping back in. Evangeline should be here. I just wanted my sister to be here.

And I feel so selfish for feeling this way. Like, how dare I decide to let myself be so bogged down right now? I'm supposed to be having fun on this trip. I'm supposed to be enjoying myself. Yet, the second I began to feel that way, it just made things worse.

After what felt like forever, the shuttle finally arrived. It would fit more than the twelve of us, so I took an empty seat toward the back, right next to the window. I was hoping that I wouldn't have to sit next to anyone during the short ride. I'm not sure I had the mental energy to be able to hold up a conversation.

But of course, nothing seems to go my way. Maybe that's a good thing. Maybe all of this was meant to happen, and Kyle was meant to sit next to me. Of course, it was Kyle who sat next to me, still wearing that ridiculous t-shirt. I wouldn't even think of anyone wanting to sit next to me when I'm in this kind of mood. I wouldn't want to sit next to me.

Kyle didn't say anything as he sat down. I was thankful for that. I was sitting, staring out the window. I wasn't even on my phone. He nudged me not too long after sitting down and held out one of his headphones. I shot him a small, thankful smile before placing the earbud into my ear. He then handed me his phone so that I could pick the music. It was like our secret language. It was his way of saying, "I know you aren't feeling great. Want to give me an idea of what's going on through music?" I knew I wouldn't be able to explain everything to him with one song. It's never that easy. So, I queued up three or four songs that I felt fully encapsulated everything I was feeling. We didn't have to say anything. Words wouldn't be able to describe everything I wanted to say to him. He shouldn't have to deal with everything that I'm going through anyway. It's not his problem that I'm such a mess.

We only got through two songs before the shuttle came to a stop, and our large group was making its way out of the shuttle and into the frozen evening air. I followed along behind. Of course, the group was splitting up into kids and adults, and the four of us, Taylor, Kyle, Perri, and I, were off to explore town and get dinner on our own. How wonderful. I should have been more excited to spend time with my friends. Since we haven't been skiing together, I barely get to see them during the day. The only person I have actually gotten to spend time with is Perri. Not that I would say that's a bad thing; I've had more fun now than I've had in a while, but there's a comfort in being with the people who have seen me at my lowest at a time where I just really need them.

We ended up walking in groups of two down the sidewalk. Kyle and Taylor led the way with Perri and I trailing along behind. Perri's warm body next to me was comforting, but there was a part of me that wished it was Kyle. I just wanted to be with someone who completely understands how I'm feeling in the moment, and who understands exactly what I need. Kyle is normally that person for me. I know that there will be a day when he isn't, or a day where he isn't the only person who knows me in that way, but right now all I need is someone who does.

"How'd your parents decide to send you on this trip? I'm sure spending time with your aunt, uncle, and cousin was how you pictured your winter break," I asked Perri quietly. When she didn't respond at first, I thought maybe she didn't hear me. That would have been fine. I would have continued to walk in silence with the knowledge that I did try to start a conversation, even if it was a halfhearted attempt.

"I think they just wanted me out of the house and felt like this was their only option. But really, I think my mom just wants to be able to go out to bars with her friends and get drunk without having any other responsibilities. And my dad's moving out. He found a new apartment a few weeks ago with his girlfriend. My mom's been pretty heartbroken about it. So why not give me to her brother for a week? I don't know if she'd care what happened to me anyway. And it's not like my father would go ahead and actually do anything." She let out a dry laugh. "He's moved in with his pregnant secretary. He got her pregnant, in case you were wondering. So, he's off trying to start this new family and forget all about the one he's leaving behind. At least I'll get to enjoy myself before I go home and have to pick up the pieces of whatever week she's had while I was away. How fun."

I was shocked at how open she seemed to be with me. We've barely known each other more than a few days, and she's already pouring her heart out to me. "I'm so sorry, that must be so hard." I tried comforting her, but honestly, I wasn't sure how.

I looked at Perri and then Kyle and Taylor to see if they'd heard any of what Perri had just said. It looked like they hadn't. I didn't know how to respond. I was trying to come up with the best response to Perri opening her soul up to me. I wanted to be comforting; she was clearly going through so much, and this trip was probably the last place she wanted to be.

"Sorry I didn't mean to dump that on you. You have enough to deal with. I just haven't been able to reach either parent for like this whole trip and it's just getting really frustrating. Sorry. I should just stop talking now." A small blush crept up onto her cheeks, and she looked down at her feet as we waited at a light to cross the street. When I realized Kyle and Taylor were too engrossed in their conversation to notice that we were actually having our own little moment, I quickly grabbed Perri's hand in my own and gave it a good squeeze. I could only hope it would convey everything I needed it to.

"I don't mind listening. Everyone has their own problems

and it's kind of nice to get a break from my own problems. You don't need to tiptoe around me because of my sister's death. I'm a big girl; I can handle whatever this world wants to throw my way." Perri laughed, and her smile was bright enough to make me forget everything that was overwhelming me.

Before I knew it, we were at the restaurant where we were going for dinner. It was a small, fast-food-like place. The perfect place for a group of teenagers. We went up to the counter with the stipends we were given from our parents, and Perri shyly stood behind us.

"What do you think you're going to get? I love the chicken sandwich here," I asked her with a smile.

"I'm not sure. I don't know if I'm going to be able to have enough money for lunches toward the end of the week if I get anything too big. My mom said she'd give me money for food when she sent me with my uncle, but I think she forgot. I just have what I've been making this year working at my local bookstore since I needed to get out of the house. I was trying to save it for spending money in college since I know she's not going to give me any, and I'll probably end up getting at least one job, but I'm starting to run out of that money. I didn't expect meals to be that expensive here."

"Let me cover your dinner tonight. Get whatever you want." I smiled in a way that I hoped would come across as flirty.

"I can't ask you to do that."

"It's not my money. And it's not like my parents would notice anyway, they normally have to pay for another kid on this trip anyway. Even if it's just the one meal, they will prob- ably still think they saved a lot of money only having one child to pay for."

Kyle and Taylor turned and gave me the strangest looks. "That's a bit harsh, isn't it?" Taylor said while Kyle remained quiet. He probably didn't want to get involved in this. I don't blame him, it's a lot for any person to deal with.

"My dad jokes about it all the time, why can't I? I'm the one with the dead sister, remember?" That shut them up pretty quickly. "Plus, you know how my parents view their money; it wouldn't make a difference if they were paying for three children. I doubt they'd even notice. And with how guilty they've been feeling lately, I could get away with anything. My dad practically hands me his wallet every time he sees me crying since Evangeline died. It's kind of funny. I know he's grieving in his own way, and we all have our own ways of dealing with all of this, but I think my emotions scare him." All of my friends looked at me with shock written all over their faces, and before I could say anything else, our food was ready.

When Kyle and Taylor turned back around to try to decide what they wanted to eat, I leaned in really close so that only Perri could hear and whispered into her ear, "besides we can treat it like a date." A small blush crept up across her cheeks as she smiled.

Chapter Twelve

There was always one night of Chanukah that I would look forward to more than the others. For the past few years, it seems like the third night of Chanukah has always been the most important. For me, it's the night when my favorite Chanukah tradition takes place. I don't remember how old I was when it all started, but I will forever remember it as the year we couldn't get an Elf on the Shelf. Why couldn't we get one, you ask? We're Jewish. It's really that simple, but when Evangeline was little, it was the one thing she had a hard time understanding. "Why does everyone else get to have one?" She would always ask with tears in her eyes. Honestly, I felt bad for her. She just wanted to fit in. But no matter how much my parents tried to explain the differences in religion and beliefs to her, she still wanted one. For her, it wasn't about beliefs or religion; it was about fitting in. Our parents had to come up with something to stop her crying. I would have done everything after she kept at it for two weeks, but they were clever and found what they thought was the perfect solution. Enter the Mensch on the Bench, the Jewish version of Elf on the Shelf for Chanukah. Same idea, different religion.

But the "magic" of it all was quickly broken when Evangeline decided he would be her new best friend and was never leaving her side. Perfect. If she had to go as far as putting him down to go take a bath, she would throw a fit. And of course, being the evil big sister I was at the time, I thought stealing it and wrapping it as one of her Chanukah presents would be absolutely hilarious. Spoiler alert: I was wrong. I was the only one who thought it was funny. My parents turned the house upside down trying to find that disgusting thing, and of course, it was nowhere to be found since it was sitting in the pile of Chanukah presents. Except, I had gotten things confused and instead of sitting on her pile as the present was supposed to, it was sitting on mine. How weird would it have looked if I had tried to move it? There was no way I was doing anything that would throw any suspicions in my direction. If my parents found out the truth, I would have been in big trouble and I wasn't risking that over what I thought was a silly little prank.

On the third night of Chanukah that year, I decided to open the present that I had accidentally wrapped for myself. Though I'm not sure I would say it was really much of an accident. But to this day, no one knows the truth. And that same night, because she had my parents believing she was absolutely shattered by the loss of her best friend, she opened a brand-new Mensch on the Bench doll in all of its beautifully packaged glory. She might have gotten into a little bit of trouble for "gifting" me her old one in an attempt to get a new one. At least that's what my parents still believe happened.

The next year, as a joke, we both ended up gifting each other our mensches. But then hers (the original one) suffered a major beheading by the neighbor's dog. When we got the news that he wasn't going to make it, I ever so graciously gave her mine. In place of my mensch, since it was now my sister's and I didn't have one of my own, my parents gifted me an Ask Bubbe doll.

A few years later, Taylor wanted in and joined us with none other than Dreidel Dog. When Kyle joined our friend group not too long after, he had to join in on the fun and brought my favorite addition to the club, Mitzvah Moose. Then, to make things more complicated, we started drawing from a hat to find out who would get which toy. To this day, Kyle still hasn't gotten the mensch.

But this year, Evangeline's not here, and I'm holding two stuffed animals. The one Evangeline was supposed to give to Kyle, and the one I was supposed to be gifting Evangeline. Yet, we're still a group of four people, and I could always just give one to Perri. Kyle's been wanting to include her more in everything we've been doing anyway. So, why not include her in this little tradition?

When it came time to open gifts, I was nearly buzzing with excitement. Kyle decided to start, passing a gift bag to Taylor. Without saying anything, Taylor passed her bag over to me. There I sat with the two bags in my hands. I handed the first one to Kyle, making sure he wouldn't be getting the mensch, and then handed the other to Perri.

Taylor and Kyle exchanged looks with each other, and while Kyle was smiling, Taylor looked as if she was about to explode. She was nearly vibrating with the anger that was bubbling up inside her.

Kyle opened his to find Mitzvah Moose tucked neatly inside and, of course, looked quite disappointed. He made some stupid comment about how "the mensch can't seem to get a year with our mensch." He refers to himself as our mensch even though he's the only one that sees any resemblance between the two, but whatever makes him happy, I guess.

Taylor then grabbed my arm and pulled me into the nearest bathroom, locking the door behind us. "What the hell was that?!" she yelled in a whisper. I tried to play dumb and gave her my best confused look before simply asking, "What?"

She sighed and gave me the look she gives her brothers when they've disappointed her. "Don't play dumb. You and I both know exactly what you did. And you didn't even have the decency to at least give Kyle and me a heads up. What has gotten into you?" She closed the lid on the toilet and sat down. "You've never acted like this before. When we let Kyle in on the mensch and friends tradition, we debated with Evangeline for three months before voting on it because she wasn't sold on having him be part of it and now you're going and replacing her with some random girl you just met. What the fuck is going on with you?"

I was shaking. Taylor has never been the best with emotions, but this was more than I was expecting from her. "I kissed her!" I blurted out without meaning to. My hands rushed to cover my mouth as I stood there, eyes wide with disbelief. "And besides, it's just some stupid tradition and you weren't even there for the start of it, so I don't under-stand what's got you so upset. You joined in on it after the fact, just like everyone else who's part of it now. I'm the only person that was actually there at the start of this. Grow up."

I turned and unlocked the door to the bathroom, leaving Taylor standing there with her mouth wide open, not sure of what her next move was going to be. I didn't hear her come up behind me, but I did feel her whip me around and slap me across the face. She had tears streaming down her face, and before I could say anything, she turned and ran out of the hotel room. I knew better than to follow. Kyle looked between the open door and me, standing, staring at it, clutching my cheek in my hand. My mom rushed over to me with ice, and that was when I realized I had bitten down on my lip pretty hard and had split it open. Kyle then turned and went to go find Taylor.

The next morning, I was woken up by my mother coming in and sitting on my bed next to me. She was holding a steaming cup of tea for me. She looked almost scared to talk to me. I knew she probably didn't know what I was going to say and how I was going to react. After last night, I honestly wasn't sure either. I've never acted like that before, and I definitely didn't mean to hurt Taylor like that.

"Taylor's out in the living room if you're ready to talk to her," my mom said softly as she brushed my messy hair out of my face with her fingers.

I looked down at the cup of tea in my hands. The last thing I wanted to do was get up out of bed and deal with whatever was going to happen when I finally talked to Taylor. But I couldn't hide out in my room forever; I would need to get out of bed and face her soon enough.

"I know I don't know anything about what's going on between the two of you, and you don't have to share any of it with me, but I think you need to remember that we are all hurting in our own ways. I know it's been hard for you, sweetie. But you're not the only one."

I know my mom was just trying to help, but she just made me feel so much worse. Everyone is going through this together, and all I've been doing is making it about me and my feelings. She's not wrong that everyone is going through it together, but it just seems like they don't care about Evangeline, at least not in the way I do. They aren't going through every turn on the mountain thinking about what she would have to say about their form, or the conditions that day, or what she would look like skiing down the run. No one else is thinking of the jokes she would be making each time I fall, or wondering how much of a garage sale her falls would be this year. No one is feeling it in the same way that I am. And I know we're all supposed to be going through this differently, but she was my sister. To everyone else, except my parents, she was just a friend or just another part of this trip. They didn't know her in the way we did.

And Taylor, of all people, having an issue with it now is just insane. Maybe she should have cared when she was needed. When I needed her support as I buried my little sister. She couldn't even do the bare minimum when I was at my lowest, and Kyle kept making all of those excuses for her. If I didn't know better, I would have assumed he was on her side. Anyone would. She could claim to be my best friend all she wants, but she got so distant after my sister's death it was like she wasn't even there. I just needed her to be there. I didn't know it would be so hard to have her there when I needed her.

I walked out into the living room and honestly was not in the mood to have much of a conversation with her, but at the very least, I should hear her out. So, I let her speak. I sat and listened.

"I shouldn't have slapped you last night. That I know. I'm not a child, I have better self-control, and I'm sorry I took my frustrations out on you in that way. There's just been so much changing lately. We're about to graduate. And graduating means we're going to be leaving each other. I know we always dreamed about going to college together, but at some point, I think those dreams changed for me. I started looking at schools in California."

California. She was planning on moving across the country and leaving me behind and didn't even think to tell me? I got up from my perch on the couch and made my way to the kitchen to start making something to eat. I needed to keep my hands busy.

"You know how much I've always loved being out there, and well, I applied early decision to UCLA. I know I shouldn't have hidden that from you. It was stupid to even think that it might be a good idea. Honestly, I didn't think I had a shot of getting in. But I got in, two weeks ago, and

I'm going. I should have told you sooner, I know. I'm sorry."

I looked at her with tears in my eyes and knew exactly how I needed to respond. "I never meant for it to come off like I was trying to replace her. I had picked her name last year when we drew from the hat. I didn't know what I was supposed to do with Dreidel Dog since he was meant to be handed to her last night. If I didn't give it to anyone, it would throw off the balance. And I know the part you are upset about is not that I gave it to Perri, it's that I didn't talk to you about it first. I should have thought about that and I'm sorry. But things with Perri are going really, really well. I'm sorry I didn't tell you sooner, but this is all kind of new and we're still trying to figure it out."

She looked like I had slapped her across the face, and while I didn't intend to have this argument with her ever, let alone on this vacation (well, this was supposed to be a vacation), I couldn't help but be hurt by her surprise. Did she really not see that coming? What did she expect from me? Actions speak louder than words, and things just weren't adding up.

"I guess we've both been pretty good at hiding things from each other lately," she said with tears streaming down her face. "And I know Evangeline was your sister, but we're all like one big family. Even though you might not see it, we've all been grieving too."

I had tears streaming down my cheeks as I ran over to give her a hug. What else are you supposed to do when your best friend just reveals the biggest secret she could possibly hold? And of course, in that moment, my mom walks in completely oblivious to the heartfelt moment we're having.

"There's no use getting ready to go skiing, girls. The mountain's closed due to the strong winds. We're taking the day off." And the two of us just started laughing. For the first time in months, things between Taylor and me felt normal.

Chapter Thirteen

A day off skiing could mean a million different things to a million different people. I'm still not sure what it means to me. In the past, we've planned our days off and filled them with lots of fun excursions and shopping trips in town, but this year we've been thrown for a loop. We had nothing planned for our day off anyway, but this was unprecedented.

Not too long after my mom left Taylor and me alone in the living room, we both got a text from Kyle asking what hot chocolates we wanted from Murdock's since he was picking up. I texted back immediately. I always get the Nutella one, though I can never remember the name of it. Taylor loves the Twix hot chocolate and gets that one every time.

I'd love to say that this is a tradition of our annual ski trips: playing video games, that is. But though it does happen quite often, it's not every year that the mountain closes due to weather. Though maybe it would be nice if it would. Maybe it would be nice to have a forced day off where we have nothing else planned. Where the only plan is being together in whatever way we see fit.

It wasn't long before both of my wonderful friends were

sitting in my living room, hooking up Kyle's Nintendo Switch to the TV. I would have thought he would have an easier time setting it up, since he's done it for the past couple of years every time we come here, but he seems not to know how to do it. I should've known this would happen. It always does. Somehow, in the span of a year, Kyle completely forgets how to set up his Nintendo Switch so that we can play Mario Party, or whatever game we seem to be obsessed with that year, during whatever free moment we seem to find.

After what feels like an eternity, Kyle finally sets up the game on the TV. He passes out controllers to all of us as we make ourselves comfortable on the couch. I sit, nestling comfortably into Perri's side on one end of the couch, while Taylor and Kyle sit on the opposite end, leaning forward in a very competitive stance.

Kyle goes through the basic setup of the game, making sure all the settings are set in a way that is best for us all, and then comes time to choose our characters. Without a second of hesitation, Kyle chooses Donkey Kong. I can't help but laugh at how predictable a move like that was. He always plays as Donkey Kong, and on the off chance that I get to the character first, and I have, he is willing to fight whoever decides they need the character over him. He did tackle me the last time I tried to play as Donkey Kong. Never again will I make that mistake.

"It's like he thinks we're going to take Donkey Kong from him," Perri laughs in my ear as she selects Daisy.

"Probably because I did try that once," I whisper back with a laugh as I select Princess Peach. "Never again. I don't need him tackling me to convince me to choose a different character. He can have Donkey Kong if he's that desperate."

Perri dissolves into a fit of giggles beside me as Taylor selects Rosalina. Kyle leans over and peers at us, his gaze harsh yet in a joking tone. "Sharing secrets over there, are we?" he asked, and we just started laughing harder. "We can share secrets too, you know," he said looking at Taylor before leaning over to whisper in her ear something that could only have been "pst pst pst pst pst." Yet that only makes us laugh harder.

"Okay, if you two are going to keep this up," Kyle shot us a look that could only be described as annoyed but loving, "we're going to play as teams. Perri and Aubrey, the two of you against Taylor and me." He smirked. He clearly thought he was such hot shit that we would panic at the thought that we would be separated into teams.

"Deal," I said with a smile, trying to match the intensity of his. "Game on." Perri dissolved into another fit of giggles into my shoulder as the game began. Our twenty-turn game started with each of us rolling our dice to decide the order of the turns. Though this might not seem like that big of a deal, on the board we were playing on, the order was everything. I rolled a lucky number seven, Perri rolled a three, Taylor rolled a five, and we all laughed as Kyle rolled a one.

"Looks like daddy's bark is stronger than his bite!" I said in a fit of giggles as my first turn began. I rolled a ten right off the bat. I watched my character move through the board, landing on an item space. This rewarded me with a cute little mushroom. When I eventually decide to use it, it will add five to whatever I roll. That will come in handy eventually. At least I hope it will. It should.

Next was Taylor's roll. She rolled a five, earning her a lucky space. She got ten coins from the lucky space and then ended her turn. Perri then rolled a four, landing on a blue space and earning herself three coins. We all sat on the edge of our seats as Kyle rolled his dice. He rolled a seven. He seemed to be vaguely happy with it, and that was a good start. He landed on a blue space just like Perri, and earned three coins.

Then came the first minigame: Hammer Drop. Being a

minigame I'm not very good at, I almost immediately dove off the edge, though it wasn't on purpose. Kyle, as always, was convinced he was going to win. But Perri stole the first win from him with her sly smile and an insane amount of focus. And there our next turns began. I rolled an eight, saving my mushroom for when I would want to use it later. Even as I passed that first star, I didn't have enough coins to get my first star.

Honestly, I was just happy as long as Kyle wasn't in the lead. I know how awful that sounds, trust me, I do, but when Kyle's in the lead, he gets sort of cocky. Besides, it's more fun to watch him boast about how great he is and then fail instead of becoming the cocky jerk he'll become if we just let him get away with whatever he wants. It's better for everyone else this way. My eight then took me to a blue space, and I collected my three coins, watching carefully as my friends followed with their turns. Even if anyone had gotten close to the star, they didn't have enough coins to be able to get their first star. It was only a matter of time before one of us would possess a chomp call and move the star right out of someone's grasp. The only person who might be close was Perri, and since we're a team, I'm not complaining. As long as Kyle loses, I'll be happy.

Perri won the next minigame as well: Flash Forward. It's not one I would consider myself to be terrible at, but I don't really think I'm good at any of the minigames. After a few turns, Taylor and Perri seemed to be making the same rolls, and Taylor jokingly shot Perri a lighthearted, "Can you please stop copying me? I know you wish you could be me, but this is just excessive."

To which Perri replied, biting back a laugh, "I don't think anyone would want to be you, but I'm glad you feel that way." I muffled a giggle into her shoulder as I began my next turn. Perri had taken the lead quite quickly, and Kyle just seemed to be running quickly behind. It was as if he was trying to catch up to her, but not quite making it. He was holding second place for what felt like the longest time.

Eventually, the game came to an end. Perri was in the lead with three stars, Kyle was right behind her with two, and Taylor and I were both trailing along with one each (though I did have more coins, earning me the third-place slot).

Then it came to the bonus stars. Perri was given one for the most minigame wins. Kyle was not a fan of that at all. I was then given the unlucky star, as if the game was laughing at me for having the star pulled out of my grip almost every time I got close to it. I guess that was what I got for going first. I gave everyone a chance to be able to pull the star from me at the very last second. Kyle had the upper hand in that regard, though I wouldn't tell him. I then was also gifted the Bowser space star because, of course, with my unluckiness, I also ended up landing on every Bowser space on the board at least once, if not more than once.

And that brought us to the end of the game. The real question was whether I had managed to usurp the win with those two bonus stars. I could have gotten that lucky, but I didn't want to believe that I had. I did want to give Perri the win.

In last place came Taylor. No one was surprised, and she just laughed as we watched her character get pulled away. Then in third place was Kyle, to no one's surprise except his own. He seemed to be really disappointed by the turn of events. He really thought he was going to win, or at the very least, get pretty close to winning. While Perri and I had already won, we waited eagerly to see who made it into second place. I had assumed it would be me, but I watched with a strangled amusement as Daisy got pulled off the screen, leaving Princess Peach as the winner. Leaving me as the winner. My first and immediate thought was to go and rub it in Kyle's face. Out of everyone in this group, I was the winner. Instead, I just called out as I made my way into the kitchen to grab one of the many boxes in the cupboard, "Winner picks dinner!"

I pulled a couple of boxes of my favorite Manischewitz Latke Mix. Now, this is quite the controversial opinion, but this latke mix tastes like childhood and everything good in the world. Every year when Evangeline and I were little, we would make latkes with my mom using this mix. And who doesn't love fried potatoes, even if they do start out as some odd-looking powder in a box?

Listen, I completely understand everyone who thinks that homemade latkes out of real potatoes are better. I get that. It's real food instead of whatever processed crap I prefer to put into my body, but every time I've ever had homemade latkes, they are just never as good as the boxed powder stuff. That's just my opinion.

I pulled down a couple of bowls and got to work. I was making these latkes whether or not anyone else was going to eat them. Well, everyone would have to; they would be our only option for dinner. I was making quite the large batch. Kyle joined me in the kitchen as Taylor put music on. We moved around the kitchen easily as we assembled our ingredients and began to make our latkes.

I beat two eggs for every box of mix we were using in the bowl while Kyle got a few cups of water. I then added the latke mix as he added water, and we mixed it all together to have a nice, large bowl of latke mix.

"Can you at least tell us what you're making?" Kyle whined from his spot on the couch. "Maybe we can help!" I just laughed and went back to my bowl. Making the latkes was like second nature to me. I was so used to it, I didn't even have to think about how to make them. Every movement was down to muscle memory. I had thrown away the box, God forbid Kyle tried to figure out what I was making. It was my secret, mine alone, and it would stay that way until I was done if I could help it. Kyle was determined. I appreciated his determination, but it wasn't getting past me. He sat down at the counter right in front of me and did all he could to stare into my soul and try to get me to crack.

"You should be able to tell what I'm making by now. Can't you see it? It's so obvious!" I teased. The bowl of mush that I was mixing wasn't going to give away any clues. But if he knew me well enough, he'd know what it was. It should have been obvious enough.

"Because I can tell what a bowl of mush is going to become," he retorted. He was clearly in a mood from losing the game, and I wasn't helping by keeping this very small secret from him.

"Come on. Use context clues. Sure, the bowl of mush might not be the best indicator of what I'm making, but what's on the counter? What have I taken out to use? That should give you at least some clue." I nodded toward the tubs of sour cream and applesauce that I had placed on the counter not too far from him.

"Now you have to let me help," he said with a smirk. I knew he was right. "I'll keep it between us. I don't think they'll even notice." I considered for a minute. I knew he was right, but I wasn't going to make this easy for him. There was no way. That would simply be too easy. I needed to see he wanted it. "I'll even make your famous spiced applesauce. We both know this generic stuff won't do." He whispered the last bit, reading my mind, and it became quite clear to me that I wouldn't be able to get everything done in a reasonable amount of time.

"Fine," I replied reluctantly. "But don't let the others know anything."

"I wouldn't dare, buttercup." If Kyle wasn't one of the gayest people I knew, I might have thought he was flirting with me, but he's just always called me the most outlandish of nicknames. My best friend was just crazy like that.

As I continued to make the latkes, I kept looking over at

Kyle and monitoring his progress with the applesauce. I knew I was probably being overbearing. I've taught him how to make my grandma's spiced applesauce. "Stop acting like we haven't done this together half a million times," he said when it became clear I was paying more attention to him than to what I was doing. I put my hands up in a defensive position and just laughed as I went back to the latke mix and the pan on the stove that was almost warm enough for me to start cooking—well, more like frying—the latkes.

It didn't take long for me to get into a comfortable rhythm standing in front of the stove. The making of the latkes was something I had been doing my whole life. Though I would always use the recipe just in case, I practically had it memorized and could make the latkes with my eyes closed.

Kyle was deeply focused on my grandmother's spiced applesauce recipe. He's been making it with my family for almost as long as I have, yet I'm still wary of allowing him to make something so special. This recipe is one that was always Evangeline's favorite. I still don't understand why she couldn't seem to enjoy latkes with sour cream, but that's her own problem. She didn't even like them with the store-bought applesauce my parents would buy when we were little and Grandma wasn't around to make her applesauce for us. My parents didn't question it when Evangeline would eat her latkes with ketchup (even though that is an abomination and anyone who does that must be mentally disturbed), but when Grandma saw that, she was in such a state of shock that she would have done anything to "make things right." She insisted on making her own applesauce for Evangeline in the middle of dinner. My parents were mortified as she got up and went to the stove in the middle of dinner to make her applesauce for Evangeline. But Evangeline loved it. If she could, I'm sure Evangeline would have eaten the entire tub of applesauce if our parents let her.

This year, Chanukah feels different. Even making latkes

feels different. I guess I should have expected it to be without Evangeline, but I didn't even think my favorite holiday meal would be so tainted by the loss of my sister. Not tainted. That's not the right word. There's just this immense feeling of wrongness around doing anything Chanukah-related without her by my side. While I love Kyle to death, it should be Evangeline next to me making Grandma's spiced apple sauce. The second I started mixing up the latke mix, she would've known what I was making without even looking at it. Maybe that's just the kind of sister she was. She knew everything before I even had the chance to tell her. She could tell by the way I was breathing what I was doing.

I bet in another life, we were meant to be twins. Maybe we were supposed to be twins in some weird way. It feels as though we were always destined to be close. We were meant to be sisters. I've had tons of best friends, but no one will ever understand me the way she did.

Kyle finished with the applesauce just as I pulled the last latke from the stove and gently placed it on top of the large pile that had accumulated on the plate.

Chapter Fourteen

While Kyle and I finished cooking, Perri and Taylor got to setting the table. Luckily for us, it would only be the four of us for dinner. The parents decided they were going to go out to dinner and get one night of dinner without the children at the table, and Taylor's parents decided to just order in pizza for Taylor's brothers. Honestly, it's probably for the best. I don't see those boys wanting to do more than just sit around playing their video games anyway. That's all they seem to want to do when they're not skiing, and for us, that meant we wouldn't have to deal with anyone getting in our way of a nice dinner as the small group of friends that we were.

We all sat around the table, me in between Perri and Kyle, sitting across from Taylor. Everyone began to eagerly fill their plates with latkes, sour cream, and my grandma's famous applesauce made by Kyle himself. Well, everyone except Perri, who was looking very uncomfortable sitting next to me.

"Do you want some?" I whispered to her as everyone else seemed to be too engrossed in their own plates to realize there was nothing on hers. She started fidgeting with the rings she wore on her left hand, refusing to meet my eyes.

"I'm good. I'm not really hungry." I could tell she was lying, but I also didn't think it was fair to blatantly call her out on her lie. "Besides, I don't really like latkes that much anyway."

Everyone at the table froze and looked at her. My fork clattered onto my plate, sending the bits of latke that were on it flying. How could she not like latkes? If there was one food I could eat for the rest of my life, it would be potatoes, and at least half the time, I'd be making latkes. I've always been team latke in the biannual hamantaschen latke debate, no matter how many people oppose me. I get it, cookies are delicious, especially the ones with fillings, but you can put virtually anything on a latke, though if you are going to do that, maybe call it a potato pancake because there are certain things (like ketchup) that when put on a latke just feel so wrong.

"I've never heard of anyone not liking latkes. I mean, I guess there was a time when my sister didn't like them, but then my grandma made her spiced apple sauce, and the rest was history. And well, look at that, Kyle made her recipe just for all of us. Why don't you give it the tiniest of tries? You can have a bite of mine. If you don't like it, we can always order something in for you, but if you do, then you can have as many as you like."

Perri really seemed to mull over my suggestion. After a few minutes of deliberation, she smiled and took my fork, which had a small piece of latke with some of the applesauce on it, and smiled at me as she took her first bite. Her eyes grew wide as she shoved the fork back into my hand and reached for her own, filling her plate with more latkes than I had seen anyone do for their first plate. Well, maybe I had seen Kyle do that, but he doesn't count. Then she grabbed the spoon in the applesauce and plopped the biggest spoonful right in the middle of the plate on top of the latkes she had piled on and began to stuff her face. I think that was the moment I fell in love with her.

I know it sounds crazy. She shoved a ton of latkes into her face and ate an insane amount of them, but it was beyond endearing to watch. Actually, it was pretty cute to watch. Whoever had made latkes for Perri in the past had clearly made bad latkes, and I was beyond thrilled to have finally shown her how amazing latkes can be.

After we finished eating, we all made our way outside. There would be no better way to end such a great night than with s'mores by the fire pit outside as it was snowing. Big, fat snowflakes were falling from the sky as we made our way to the fire pit. It wasn't too far from our room. S'mores have always been one of my favorite traditions, though it's one that somehow tends to be the first to be forgotten.

Maybe "forgotten" wasn't the best word. I wouldn't say that Evangeline ever really loved going out for s'mores. No matter how close to the fire she sat, she was always way too cold, and she hated marshmallows, so she wasn't even eating the s'mores. She would just spend the whole evening outside complaining about how cold it was, and while she had every right to complain, it wasn't fair to the rest of us who wanted to be there more than anything. Well, maybe that was just me. But s'mores by the fire pit have always just been so cozy and such a nice way to end a fun and chill day like today.

I was weird sitting around the fire pit without Evangeline there to complain about the cold. It made me realize how little we would actually talk to each other when we were out here. I guess we'd talk, sure, but half the time we'd be joking around with Evangeline saying things like "it's not that cold" or "why don't you just jump in the fire then?" Without her here, I want to hate the cold as much as she did. I can't bring myself to do it though. I've always preferred the cold. Evangeline would always say I was crazy.

Perri brought out her guitar, the one thing I was shocked that she wanted to bring on this trip. Don't get me wrong, I don't think bringing it was a bad idea; I just never thought we'd have time for her to play. These trips can feel quite chaotic. Guitar practice isn't something that has ever gotten prioritized before. But out here, while sitting by the fire roasting marshmallows and just enjoying being in each other's company, it couldn't have felt more right. Perri was playing music I could only refer to as my youth group favorites. They weren't songs that were inherently Jewish or any kind of prayer; they were just songs that came up a lot during youth group song sessions, and I have tied them to my love for my youth group ever since.

Perri looks so at peace sitting on the comfy chair next to the fire pit. Her long ginger curls are tucked neatly under her lavender beanie. She had tied most of her hair back into a low ponytail, presumably to get it out of the way, but a few strands fell from the ponytail to frame her face. It was odd how in the cold, I could see her resemblance to Kyle. I've known that they're related, but there was something about seeing them next to each other, the way both of their cheeks had become flushed in the cold, and the matching pattern of freckles across their noses that really brought their resemblance together.

We didn't light the Chanukah candles that night. I don't think anyone really noticed that we hadn't. I guess I was the only one who did. In past years, I wouldn't have cared if we didn't light the candles. It was never something that had ever felt like a big deal to me. There were always nights when we would be too busy or too wrapped up in our own worlds to remember that we needed to take a few minutes to light the candles. When we were little kids, there was no way we would miss a single night. That was back when we would get eight presents, one for every single night of Chanukah. As kids, the most important part of the holiday was the presents. We never really cared about the food or traditions or anything else that makes a holiday feel like a holiday. Back then, if I was told Chanukah was just the Jewish Christmas, I would have agreed. To me, that was all it was. But then I grew up, got involved with a youth group, and took a deeper understanding of religious practices and what Chanukah truly meant. I fell in love with the resilience of the Jewish community that Chanukah, like many of our holidays, aims to celebrate.

Chapter Fifteen

This was going to be fun. And a great way to take the stress off me. I hope she's done some research. I was honestly glad to be able to take a break and not have to think and plan. If Perri was taking care of the planning for the day, I didn't have to worry about having to think of fun and different things we could do to keep the skiing new, fresh, and fun. Especially since I am the kind of person who has the runs and areas that I love and that I love to stick to. I have a hard time branching out and trying new things and new runs.

We all met up at the Orange Bubble lift. We then got in line for the lift and made our way up. I was eager to see what my day would look like. Perri had the whole day and all of the runs planned out (or at least I hoped she did).

We skied down to the Red Pine base area, and then it was up to Perri. My fate and the fate of the day were in her hands.

The day started like the rest we've seen, just like the day before, with Snow Dancer. Being so early, the run hadn't been skied down too much and was rather empty. For it being one of the first runs of the day, it went relatively smoothly. Roughly halfway down the run, Perri veered onto Flying Salmon. I just followed; that was simply the plan for the day. My fate was in her hands, and I wouldn't have it any other way.

When we made our way down to the bottom of the run, Perri led me back over to Saddleback. We got in line for the lift once again.

"So, what's the plan this time?" I asked, eager to gain some sort of understanding of the plan for the day, but not trying to push too hard.

"It's a surprise," Perri replied simply, without turning to face me.

"What? You're not even going to give me the slightest hint?" I leaned closer toward her as we moved up in line, gently bumping her arm.

"The lift is hint enough." She smirked, and I noticed her look down to my lips for half a second. Was she thinking about the kiss? We haven't even addressed it. But she kissed me, so she must like me, right? But what does that make us? Are we dating? Is she my girlfriend? Does she even want that? And what's going to happen when we get home from this trip? Is this even something that's going to last beyond the trip?

My thoughts were interrupted when it was our turn to get on the chairlift. All of my focus went to getting onto the lift. Not that it's a difficult task, but if you're not paying attention, the chair can come up behind and just smack you right in the butt, and that's never fun.

When we got to the top of the lift, I followed Perri off, sliding my wrists into the straps on my poles, as she made her way to the right-hand side; to Kokopelli. I followed cautiously, knowing my history with the run isn't the best. As she turned onto the run, I followed, making sure to follow in her tracks. If I focused hard enough on just trying to match her tracks during the steep part of the run, then I would be fine. As long as I wasn't focusing on the terrain I was skiing and focused on the skiing instead, I was going to be fine.

Once we made it past the steep part, my confidence reached a new high. I ended up passing Perri, making my way down the run until I got to the split where I stopped and waited for her.

"Damn, girl! Look at that confidence!" Perri cheered as she stopped right in front of me. I just smiled in response and hoped she didn't notice me blushing.

She then led me down Hurricane Alley. I was rather cautious skiing down this part of the run, but I just focused on using her tracks as a guide when I felt my anxiety start to creep up again. She reminded me of skiing with my sister, and honestly, that might be pretty okay.

When we got down to the bottom of the run, Perri used the momentum we had built up as she made her way over to Chicane. This made skiing the flat part at the beginning of the run a bit easier. And with this surge of confidence I had found, skiing the run came easier than I had anticipated.

We made it down to the Tombstone base area just in time for lunch. We grabbed a table and got food, and were not even a few seconds into eating when she got a phone call.

"Hi." I heard her speak. "I'm at lunch. What's up?" She didn't seem to be too thrilled with the call, and I could only assume she felt the same way as I did. I wanted to be talking to Perri and getting to know her, but here I was.

"Now is really not a good time, ma. Can this wait?" She sighed and got up. I wanted to follow her and hold her and be part of the moment with her, but she clearly needed space, and I was going to give that to her. I picked at the chips on my plate, waiting for her to return.

It wasn't long until she came back to the table with a sour expression on her face. I picked up my sandwich and just kept eating. I tried to meet Perri's gaze, but it was clear to me that she was trying to avoid mine.

Eventually, she looked up and made eye contact with me, and I felt something inside me shift. She just got up and left. I followed her that time. I couldn't really make myself eat at that point anyway.

"Hey, is everything okay?" I asked. I didn't realize she had been crying until she began gasping for air as she tried to respond. But I didn't even know what I wanted to say. Maybe she wants to keep this personal news personal. But isn't just bottling things up and keeping them to yourself worse for you in the end? Maybe.

"Things at home are just rough." She said as I moved to sit down next to her.

"You don't have to talk about it with me now or ever, but if you need someone to talk to, I'm here." I said with a sad smile. She just nodded. "We can sit here as long as you need."

I liked her company. I liked the way she was always so cautious around others and was so scared to say the wrong thing or push someone too far and have them say something they never wanted to. I liked the way her smile could light up an entire room and how she could make me feel like I was the only person that mattered in an entire room because she thought I had something important to say.

We just sat there for a while, her head resting on my shoulder, before getting up and heading over to our skis. We put our skis on, and Perri was leading me to the Timberline lift.

By the time we got on Iron Mountain, I couldn't bring myself to think of anything else. Perri didn't seem like herself, and even though I've only known her for a few days, something just felt off. Perri seemed to be in a sort of fog for the rest of the day. No matter what we did on the mountain, nothing seemed to be able to shake her out of it. I tried to do anything I could to start conversations, start a race, or do anything. I just wanted to get through to her, but every attempt I made was brushed off or was met with some half-hearted response.

By the end of the day, I think we were both just ready to go inside and be done for the day. The night wasn't much easier. Even though we went out to dinner, neither one of us seemed to be in much of a mood to talk. When we got to the prayers and lighting the candles, everyone was so tired we didn't even try to exchange gifts. We all just went our separate ways.

However, before Kyle had a chance to run off back to his hotel, room, I grabbed his arm and pulled him into my room.

"Dude, what's up? It's getting late, my parents will worry if I'm out any longer," Kyle said. But when he met my eyes, he just sat down on my bed.

"I'm worried about Perri. She received a call during lunch, and it made her really upset. I couldn't seem to get to her for the rest of the day; she just shut down. You're her cousin; you know her way better than I do. Maybe she'll talk to you. I'm just really worried about her."

Kyle nodded, then got up and began to leave the room. "Thanks, Aubrey. I'll handle it. I'm glad the two of you are starting to get close." He shot me a sad smile before turning to leave the room. If only he knew how close we really were.

Chapter Sixteen

I needed to talk to Perri today. We didn't have to decide to tell everyone about our relationship, but I needed to come out to Taylor and Kyle, especially Kyle. Coming out to Taylor is just really scary, but I know Kyle will love me no matter what. I mean, there isn't a reason he wouldn't, right? The thought of Kyle hating me or not talking to me because I came out would break me. And he's also pretty gay. But even if we don't get to talk about the kiss and what it meant, maybe we'll just get to talk and have fun and deal with whatever that phone call yesterday was about.

I stayed up late at night just thinking about my sexuality. I mean, I think I have liked guys before, but this is my first relationship. I was able to come to the conclusion that I was, in fact, bisexual.

As soon as I woke up, I jumped out of bed and made my way to the bathroom. I stood in front of the mirror looking at myself. If I wanted to come out to anyone else, I would have to come out to myself first, right? I stared at my face in the mirror, and it became hard for me to speak.

I didn't realize saying two words would be so hard. I just wanted to be able to say them and know that I was comfortable with the label. I just stood there, staring at myself in the mirror, waiting to be able to just say those two (or three) little words. Why was it so hard?

Maybe I just wasn't ready. The thought that I might not have been ready was seriously shocking, but I would need to take my time with this. It wasn't just something that could happen overnight. I couldn't just wake up comfortable.

But I had been spending so much time thinking about it, I could only really think that I had to be ready for it. This was just the next step. I just had to do what comes next. Why was it so fucking hard for me to just look in the mirror and come out to myself?

Time was running out, and I needed to have breakfast and get ready for the day.

After breakfast, I was back in the bathroom, staring at myself. If I didn't do it now, I would never do it, would I?

I took a deep breath, and then in a whisper, I looked at myself and said: "I'm bisexual," and it felt so good. It felt right. I looked at myself in that mirror, and everything just seemed to make sense.

I didn't realize how hard it was going to be to come out to myself. My sexuality had just been something that seemed so obvious and obviously confusing to me when I thought about it, but thinking and saying are two very different and very hard things.

But if I could come out to myself, then I should be able to come out to other people too, right? I just hope the rest of the day goes well.

When we got onto the Saddleback lift, I wanted to start my conversation with Perri, but I knew I didn't want to have it with other people on the chair with us. That might not be the best idea, not for this conversation.

I felt like I would have to wait all day to talk to Perri and to have the conversation I wanted to have with her. Maybe I would be lucky and be able to have the conversation with her before, but the odds were very unlikely. Well, that was until we headed down Chicane. Unless we took Tombstone up and skied off that lift, which wasn't something I really wanted to do anyway, then the conversation would have to wait much longer.

I began to feel lucky when Perri suggested we take Timberline and Iron Mountain and maybe ski Copperhead before lunch.

When we were on the Iron Mountain lift, I saw my opening. I mustered up all the courage I could to talk to Perri about coming out.

"Hey, I have a question for you if you don't mind me asking," I said nervously.

"What's up?" Perri responded calmly.

"How did you know you were gay? And what was it like coming out to friends? Is it as scary as I think it will be?"

"Why are you asking?"

"I've been thinking about it. I mainly just want to come out to Kyle. I won't tell them about us. I promise. Unless that's something you want to tell them about, and I don't even know what I would say. Would I just be like 'hey Kyle, by the way, I kissed your cousin.' I just feel guilty hiding so much from them. I've never hidden anything from them. Ever."

"Okay, that's completely valid! When it came to my own sexuality, I guess I just knew. I don't know how else to explain it other than that. It just made sense to me, I guess. Coming out to my friends was terrifying, and I'm sure you have the right idea of how scary it is going to be. But my friends back home are some of the most accepting people and I knew that going into it."

"I just don't know how Taylor and Kyle are going to react. I'm pretty sure Taylor is going to hate me for the rest of her life. Kyle might be more accepting, but I have nothing to go off other than the occasional homophobic comments Taylor has made in the past. But maybe my coming out would change her views on these kinds of things. But I can't be that lucky, can I?" I fidgeted with my poles anxiously.

"I wouldn't bet on it, but you never know. You might be pleasantly surprised." Perri smiled at me, and her warm smile was all that I needed.

"Maybe we should also address the kiss. If you want. I mean, it's just been a few days, and we haven't really talked about it, not that we have to talk about it, but I guess I'd just like to know what it means for us." I couldn't even look at her. I couldn't bring myself to face whatever she must have been thinking in that moment.

"Maybe that's a conversation for later. I'm not saying that's not a conversation to have, but maybe not on a chairlift that's about to reach the top." We pushed ourselves off the chair and began to ski down Copperhead.

"I have a surprise run I want to take you on after lunch," Perri said when we sat down with our food. The idea of a surprise run made me both excited and nervous. The chances of me having been down the run in the past are high, but the idea that it is a surprise would mean that it would probably be a challenge for me, and I wasn't really excited or interested in pushing myself like that again.

"Yeah? You're not going to give me any hints, are you?" I asked, hoping to get something out of her so that I could at least try to figure out what it was that we were doing.

"Nope! No hints. Besides, you did ask me a question earlier, and I think we've got some time to talk about it now." She bit into her sandwich, and I looked down at mine, my stomach filling up with anxiety at what could potentially come of this conversation. "Aubrey, I really like you."

I sat up just a little bit straighter. "I feel like there's a 'but' coming."

She locked eyes with me, and I saw a flash of something across her face. "There's no but. Aubrey, I'd love to be your girlfriend, if you'll have me."

I surveyed the group of people surrounding us, making sure Taylor and Kyle were nowhere to be seen, and then I grabbed her face and kissed her.

Chapter Seventeen

We finished up lunch, and I was both excited and nervous for the next run that Perri was going to take me on. The prospects of the run excited me, but the idea of it scared me. I don't like surprises and not knowing what is coming. I know that is part of what triggers my anxiety. I normally try to avoid surprises, but I didn't want to turn Perri down. Especially when she was so excited to take me down this run. All I could do was remind myself that I have been down all areas of the mountain and probably will know what run I'm on and what run I'm going to be going down.

"Just don't look at the signs for any of the runs and you should be fine. Do you trust me?" Perri asked me as we got off the Tombstone lift.

"Of course, I trust you," I replied with a nervous smile on my face. I hoped she didn't notice how nervous I was.

"Good. I'm glad. You just need to trust your ability to get down the run. I know it's easier said than done, but I know you have the skills to get yourself down any run you end up on." I laughed. If only she were right.

"You're not taking me down a black run, are you?"

"I wouldn't take you down something I didn't think you could handle."

I was glad when we veered to the left that she wasn't taking me down Another World. That run has caused too many panic attacks. I hate going down that run so much. Instead, we went toward the Peak 5 lift. I had done this a bunch and wasn't too nervous about it.

I only began to get nervous when we skied past the lift and kept going down. The beginning of the run we were going down, Escape, was a run that I loved. It had been so long since I had been down it, but the run was such a nice and fun one. Normally, I continue down the blue run and end up on the bottom half of Another World, but I knew that would be too easy for Perri to have chosen as a challenge for me. We would be going down one of the two other runs over there. They were both black runs. Even if I hadn't been down any one of them before, I would be very nervous. It was so hard for me not to look at the signs and learn what runs we were going down.

I just had to focus on the run ahead of me and the turns I was making. I realized that she was going to take me down the run called The Drop. Did I want to go down it? Of course not! But I didn't have much of a choice. However, I probably would freak myself out in the meantime.

"Why don't you go first?" Perri suggested. I took a deep breath and nodded. I looked out onto the run. It really didn't look that bad. Leadfoot was probably worse.

Here's my thing with The Drop. I have been down it before. It was one of the worst panic attacks I've had on the mountain (not counting Leadfoot, which was the actual worst), and that happened to be the one time I had an instructor who didn't know how to help me down it. He practically carried me down it because he didn't see another option.

I looked out onto the run and reasoned with myself. It didn't look bad, and I had been down it before. It might be icy, but that might be the only thing that keeps me from taking it. No. Nothing would keep me from taking the run. It wouldn't be as hard as I was anticipating. I could get down it.

I slowly pushed myself out onto the run. I nearly went across the whole thing before I realized I needed to make my first turn. I didn't want to get stuck again. As I thought about making the turn, my heart started beating really fast, and I knew my anxiety was beginning to set in. I just needed to push past it. If only it was that easy.

I managed to shape my skis into a wedge and make that first turn. I practically crossed the whole run before I was able to make my next turn. I just kept doing that until I was down the run. Toward the end, my turns got tighter.

"Look at you go!" Perri called from the top of the run as my turns began to get smaller, and I began to get faster. The run was somewhat icy, but it wasn't all that bad.

Perri's encouragement only made me want to be better and ski faster. I smiled as I kept making turns and made my way down the run. When I made it to the bottom of the run, back at the Tombstone base area, I was beaming.

"I'm so proud of you!" Perri cheered. Her smile was wide as she pulled her phone out of her jacket pocket. "I want to capture this moment," she said, then took a selfie of the two of us on Snapchat. She captioned it, "this girlie just went down a black run. So proud," with a smiley face.

I couldn't believe I had made it down the run without having a panic attack. Maybe this was progress, or maybe it was just my anxiety playing tricks on me. I almost did have a panic attack, but I'm glad I didn't. I really didn't want to have to deal with that today. "You knew it was a black run," didn't you?" Perri asked when we got on the lift to ski down for the end of the day. We had spent a very long time over by The Drop because it took me a while to muster up the courage to start skiing down the run, and I skied relatively slowly down the run.

"Yeah, I did. I've skied at this mountain every winter for almost the last ten years. I have a very good idea of what's out there and where the runs are. And I've been down it before. If I didn't know the mountain as well as I do, you probably would have done a better job of tricking me like that," I said with a smile.

"Yeah, probably, but on some level, it did work. You didn't panic."

"I wouldn't say that is why I didn't panic, and honestly, I did panic a little. I just tried to ignore it."

"Why do you think you were able to control it like that during this time and not the other?"

"I guess I just put this pressure on myself that I was holding you back and that we weren't getting to ski as much as you wanted to because I was letting my anxiety get the best of me, and we weren't getting to as many runs. This is why I normally ski with ski school. It's really more of a precaution than anything else, but still, there is a level of security that comes with knowing that in some capacity the instructor is being paid to deal with me. I just worry that I will get either hurt or stuck. It's really not fun."

"Has that happened before?"

"There was this one time about three or four years ago."

"What happened?"

"I was skiing with Taylor, just the two of us, and we had taken Super Condor up. I was going to take Boa, and Taylor was going down one of the black runs. She had told me the name of the run back then, but I don't really remember it now. I watched Taylor start to go down the run before I headed down on my own. Boa happened to be pretty icy, and

I just took it pretty slow. However, she had gone down pretty fast, and after about ten minutes of waiting for me, she began to worry. So, probably five minutes after Taylor got on the lift up, I made my way over to the lift, which was our meeting area. And when she wasn't there, I was worried she had gotten hurt, so I got on the lift to go try and find her."

"No, you did not!"

"I really wish I didn't. Long story short, I got really stuck on the run and started panicking really bad. The only thing that got me down the run was the idea that she was potentially hurt. I was so scared for her. We both hated each other for that, but now we look back and laugh. Although at the time it was traumatic and I had to start skiing with instructors to help me get down runs."

"I'm sure it wasn't that bad."

"Oh, it was. I looked like I was about to just roll down the mountain or something. I had to sideslip down the whole run because it was so steep. I really should never ski like that ever again."

That night, Perri and I decided to go into town, just the two of us. We promised our families we'd be back to light the candles. This was the closest we would be able to get to a date night. We had gone in relatively early, and we decided to just change and head out for a nice little afternoon trip into town. We had to be back by around seven, but that would give us plenty of time to wander around town and just spend some time together. It was going to be our first official date.

The first place we headed was Dolly's Bookstore, my favorite place in all of Park City. We stopped first at the chocolate shop for a nice snack. Their fudge is some of the best I've ever had. I look forward to it every year.

I could spend hours upon hours in the bookstore. I could walk in circles and discover new books every single time. I've found so many books that I've been intrigued by before they became popular by seeing them in Dolly's. It's one of the few things that makes me wish I lived in Park City. It would be the perfect blend of city and mountains to give me everything I could ever want. Dolly's is also just the perfect place to spend a rainy spring afternoon, that is, if I was ever present in Park City during the spring. Maybe that will be in my future. Maybe I'll move here after college, or maybe even for college. It would be the perfect place to start over where I'm not known by everyone for being the dead girl's sister or the girl whose sister killed herself. Here I could be someone worth something. Someone who isn't known for the worst thing to happen to them.

We didn't stay in Dolly's for too long. My parents would've killed me if I bought anything anyway. But Main Street was our perfect little heaven. All the lights and holiday decorations made the place exactly what we needed it to be. Honestly, it was perfect.

It was also freezing, and we had to stop for hot chocolate eventually. We didn't get to go anywhere special, just Starbucks, but even still, I got to walk through town, one hand wrapped around my warm beverage, the other intertwined with Perri's.

We walked around town for a while. We had nowhere specific to be, but it was nice just to spend some time together. The time flew by and before I knew it, we were getting on the bus and heading back to the hotel. Back to our reality. But before we left, we made sure to take as many cute pictures as we could pose for in the snow.

Back at the hotel, we spent about a half hour in the lobby. The hotel was having this little cocktail hour with hors d'oeuvres. The lobby was full of families and children running around, but with Perri by my side, I had the time of my life. We fed each other different little appetizers while we waited for Taylor and Kyle to join us.

When we finally made it back up to the hotel room, all of the parents decided it was time to celebrate the fifth night of

Chanukah. We all stood around the menorah as we lit the candles. We were officially over the halfway point of the holiday, and therefore halfway through the trip. I didn't want to leave. Being here had become so much more to me than I had expected. I had thought this was going to be just another ski trip. I thought it was going to be awful. I'd be stuck in ski school because my friends didn't want to deal with me, and I would end up being so lonely without Evangeline. My sister was always the one to ski with me or join in on the lessons with me, even though she could easily keep up with Kyle and Taylor. She would just stay back with me because she knew I needed it. She would never let me feel lonely.

Without her here, I thought I would feel the weight of her absence. I thought I wouldn't be able to make it through. She was the one person that kept me sane during these big group trips. She was the one person who could keep me from going crazy having to spend so much time with our parents and family stuff. I haven't even given any of our family stuff a second thought. Maybe that's because Evangeline isn't here. I wouldn't say she caused drama on these trips, but without her here, the family seems calmer. Maybe my parents still think I'm fragile. Maybe they don't want to even risk starting any conflicts because of how I might react. Maybe they're scared to lose me like Evangeline.

But this trip has been the best thing to have happened to me since Evangeline's death. Not that her death was a good thing; it was the worst thing that has ever happened to me. But for the first time, I find myself being happy and having fun without feeling guilty. I wish she was here to experience this. She would love Perri. I know she would. Perri is one of the coolest people I have ever met. Anyone in their right mind would fall in love with her within seconds of meeting her, and here I am getting to spend all the time in the world with her. For now.

But this trip being half over means that once this week is

done and we all go home, I may never see Perri again. She'll go back to her family and the mess that is waiting for her, and I'll be with mine. When this trip is over, she will leave, we will go home, and the magic that we've created here will be broken. When this trip is over, so is our relationship.

Chapter Eighteen

I woke up to the sound of my phone alarm going off. It felt like I was waking up early for school. I struggled to peel my eyes open as I blindly reached for my phone to shut my alarm off. I forced myself out of bed and made my way to the bathroom to pee and brush my teeth before I headed into the kitchen for breakfast with my parents.

"Morning sleepyhead!" My mom chirped as I groggily trudged into the room and sat on one of the stools. "Coffee?" she asked, and I grunted in response. She just placed a cup of coffee and a bowl of cereal in front of me.

"You look like you're about to pass out. Sleep well?" She laughed.

"Yeah. You?" I said as I began to wake up and become more and more of a person.

"I was up and down a lot. But that's kind of normal for me." She smiled and sat down beside me.

Once I had woken up a bit more, I made my way back to the bathroom with my clothes for the day and began to get ready. I was moving a bit slower than normal, but I was still determined to keep up our wonderful timing.

Once I finished getting ready, I got my boots on before

heading out to grab my skis and meet up with my amazing friends.

It wasn't long before we were in line for the Orange Bubble and were on our way up to start skiing for the day. We were so tired after getting to sleep the night before that it was hard for us to really wake up and talk to one another.

As we skied down to the base, my entire body was protesting. I was just so sore from how tense my body had been the past few days. However, as I flew down the mountain, I felt alive again. It felt like for that moment, nothing else mattered. I was flying down the mountain in complete control. It was a kind of control I hadn't experienced in such a long time.

I wasn't sure where we would be going next. Taylor and Kyle went off on their own path as soon as we got down to the Red Pine base area. I knew the mountain like the back of my hand. I had been skiing here since I was little, but when it came to choosing the run I would want to ski, I was utterly clueless. I figured it would be best for Perri to decide since she had now skied this mountain for about a week and had a general idea of all of the wonderful runs that the mountain had to offer.

She decided quickly that we should ski Snow Dancer just as we had been and then maybe head over to Tombstone or take Kokopelli. I figured that it was a good idea and just followed her lead as she made her way over to the Saddleback lift. The lift line wasn't very long this early in the morning and it seemed like a pretty good idea. Five minutes later, we were on a chair on the way up.

"So, what has been your favorite part of the trip so far?" I asked Perri, even though I probably knew what the answer was.

"Hm, let me think. You know that's actually a pretty hard question. I mean the fact that we started dating is a pretty big thing that happened on this trip, but would that be my favorite? You know I'm not sure." I rolled my eyes and she just laughed. "No, of course, it's when we started dating you loser. Did you really think I would say something else?"

"I don't know. I thought maybe the patrol dogs would have been more favorable." I smirked and bumped my shoulder against hers.

"Than you? Are you fucking kidding me? They were cute, and a close second, but you are my favorite part of this entire trip. I can't believe you actually thought otherwise. What about you? What has your favorite part been?"

"Watching Kyle not get the mensch again."

"You're joking."

"Actually no. He was so disappointed, but he should know he's never going to get it."

"I find it hard to believe that was really your favorite."

"It was!"

"I call bullshit."

"I'm being serious." I couldn't help but giggle.

"No, you're not, you idiot. You love me. You just don't want to admit it." I froze in my seat. It had only been a few days since we had first kissed.

"You really think that?" I tried to keep my voice from shaking.

"Yeah."

"Yeah?"

"I also think you really want to kiss me, but our gear is in the way. And we're on a chair lift."

"You might be right about that."

"And I also think you are totally messing with me and your favorite part of the trip was us getting together."

"Maybe."

"Maybe?"

"I'm not saying you're right but..." Teasing her was so much fun.

"I'm totally right."

"Sure."

"Yes! I win!"

"What are you winning? This wasn't a competition."

"I won your affection, duh!" She started giggling, and it was honestly the cutest thing I had seen.

The chair pulled up to the top, and we got off. Perri was still giggling as we started to make our way down Snow Dancer. Even behind her gear, her smile was bright and it made me glow.

We took the steep bit at the end of Snow Dancer and just used the momentum from that to start going down Chicane. I confidently trailed behind Perri for most of Chicane. It was always nice to take Chicane in the morning before a lot of people had been down it. It is normally less icy in the morning, and I always love when it is somewhat empty. However, Chicane is almost never empty, like most of the runs around the Red Pine area, but it gets us to some of my favorite runs and out onto the less populated areas of the mountain.

When we got down to the Tombstone lift, we got right in line. The line wasn't too long as I had seen it in the past, but it wasn't the shortest line either. The nice thing about the lift, though, is that it seats six people at once, which helps with the lines. But it is also an incredibly popular lift and one that opens up the parts of the mountain that normally have fewer people on them.

It took about ten minutes for Perri and me to get to the front of the line for a very full chair. Perri was leading today, so all I had to do was follow. I wasn't entirely sure where she wanted to go from here, but there was so much of the mountain that we hadn't been to and that we could explore. I couldn't wait to see where we were going to end up, but I knew that whatever run Perri decided to take me down would be fine and I knew that I would enjoy myself no matter what. After successfully conquering The Drop, I was more confident than I had expected to be. I wasn't sure that I would be willing to go down The Drop or another hard run like that, but I was willing to do pretty much anything else.

It wasn't long until we were getting off the chair at the top of the lift. I followed Perri as she headed down Red Pine Road. I was expecting to be going down the run since it was both the easiest run and the most crowded run, but I followed Perri without questioning it. I always loved this run even if it did tend to be more crowded. It was also a wonderful, nice, and open run. Occasionally when it was icy, I would have a bit of an issue with it, but as my confidence skiing on ice was growing, my confidence on the mountain was growing too.

I flew down the run with a descent of confidence until Perri stopped off to the side near the opening of Pinball Alley.

"Want to try it?" she asked. I didn't want to say no, but there was a part of me that maybe wanted to. I didn't have to do anything I didn't want to do. I didn't want to challenge myself and go down the difficult run, but I also didn't want to say no to Perri. I really just wanted to impress her. So of course, my dumb ass said yes.

"I'll follow you," she said, urging me to start going down the run. "I just want to make sure you're okay."

I nodded and pushed myself into the run. I had done this run so many times before, so why was I nervous this one specific time? I knew I could do it, so I just pushed myself and slowly picked my way through the run. As I gained confidence, I started to pick up the pace. I was mostly in a wedge due to anxiety, but I was almost able to pull my skis to be parallel. I say almost because as I tried to pick up one of my skis to pull them both into a parallel stance, I completely wiped out and I wiped out hard.

I'm sure it looked hilarious, and I would probably be laughing about this in twenty minutes or so, but in the moment, I was embarrassed. And my ass hurt too. I was also having trouble getting up. I couldn't straighten myself out.

"Hey, are you okay?" Perri asked as she picked up my poles, which I had lost in the fall. She put them to the side so she could help me up. My skis were sort of tangled, and there was no way I was going to be able to get up without either taking off one ski or getting help from Perri.

"Yeah. It's more shock than anything. I guess this is what I get for trying to ski more confidently." I laughed.

"Oh my god you idiot." She shoved me playfully. "Here, let me help you up." She skied in front of me and moved my legs so that it would be easier for me to push myself up. After she moved my legs, she reached out her hand, which I grabbed instantly, and pulled me up.

"That was quite some fall." She laughed. "Are you sure you're okay?"

"Yes. I promise you I'm okay. I probably just bruised my ass if anything. I'll let you know later if I did," I said with a laugh.

"Okay, weirdo, let's keep going. We're almost there." I followed her for the rest of Pinball Alley, and then we popped back out onto the tail end of Red Pine Road and skied back down to the Red Pine base area.

We then headed back over to Chicane so that we could stop at Tombstone for lunch as per usual. We both practically flew down Chicane without stopping. We even skipped the bypass for the first time. It was honestly kind of nice to change it up even though it was just a little bit. I was nervous at first since it was a lot steeper than I had anticipated, but I just picked my way down it and made it out comfortably on the other side.

We then pulled right up to the ski racks and popped our skis off to go grab some lunch. We ordered and grabbed the buzzers before we found a table and sat down.

We then started talking and just getting to know each other. We talked about anything and everything. Our conversations went from books to movies to TV shows and plays and whatever else we could think of. We talked all through lunch.

After lunch, we got our skis on and made our way back over to the Tombstone lift. At this point, we were pretty much collaborating on what our route was for the afternoon. We were both pretty good with doing whatever, so it wasn't too hard to just pick something we liked and knew well.

We headed over to lift Peak 5 and decided to take Silver Spur over to Harmony, then take all of Harmony back down to Tombstone. The run was nice, long, and incredibly relaxing. It was a run I was very confident on, and I really loved the run. I had done it so many times that my confidence just took over, and I was just skiing without even thinking about it. This confidence was something I wished I could have in my life outside of skiing. If I was this confident about everything in my life, I would be so much more successful, and maybe then I wouldn't be second-guessing myself so much or driving myself crazy over every tiny little detail. If I could just be less anxious all the time, then things would just be so much easier.

Once we got back down, we decided it might be a good idea to just do that again. With lift lines and everything, we could probably do all of Harmony one more time before we would ski down for the day. Even though the day wasn't as full as we normally had it, it was still a nice, chill day to get ourselves back into skiing as we had been before our day off.

We skied down at the end of the day. As I took my skis off and gave them to the valet, I felt the soreness of my body. With this trip being so long, I was really pushing myself more than I had expected. I couldn't wait to get back to the room and take a nice hot shower. We would be having dinner at the resort again tonight, and I was really just against Drafts again. We were having it so much; I just needed a break from it. Kyle said he and I would go to Murdocks and pick up a pizza for everyone, and I wanted one of their special hot chocolates.

They have some of the best hot chocolates with all these different fillings in them, and it's just so wonderful and warm. Their pizza isn't bad either. I'm not a huge fan of pizza, but I will eat it and I don't mind theirs.

It was pretty cold when Kyle and I walked out of the hotel and made our way over to Murdock's. I couldn't wait to have my warm hot chocolate in my hand. We had made a deal that Kyle would hold the pizza and I'd take the hot chocolates, but then I'd have to get all the doors for him on the way back. It was fair and I didn't mind it all that much.

We brought the pizza and hot chocolates back and all just hung out in the hotel room. It was a perfect scene. I love my friends sometimes more than life itself, and I just love seeing them all together and all happy. The large smiles on their faces make everything so much better. I didn't want the moment to end. Kyle was making dumb jokes, Taylor was rolling her eyes and smiling, and Perri was in a fit of laughter. She was new to Kyle's antics and was actually able to find them entertaining, unlike Taylor and I who had heard Kyle make the same stupid joke for the hundredth time. He has his jokes and he likes to reuse them even when everyone around him is totally sick of hearing the same shit every fucking day. But the way he smiles when he makes the jokes just makes it all worth it. It always looks like he's about to let us in on a secret and it's something he's never told anyone before. It's that light in his face when he tells his stupid jokes that make it worth listening to them over and over again.

After dinner, we all decided to go take a walk around Canyons Village. Perri really wanted to get some cute photos, and the sun was setting so beautifully that I don't know anyone who wouldn't want to be out there. We all practically ran outside to enjoy the night together. Perri was taking some pictures of me with the sunset and mountain as the background when I felt a cold snowball hit me in the back. I turned around to see Kyle laughing hysterically. Of course,

Kyle was the one to throw the first snowball. I looked to the nearest ledge that had snow piled on top of it, made my first snowball, and hurled it at Kyle. Before I knew it, we were pelting snowballs at each other, all hysterically laughing. Perri shrieked when a snowball got close to hitting her and ran to put her camera away in its case before joining in on the fight.

Chapter Nineteen

After our snowball fight, we ended up back in my family's condo, shivering and trying our best to get warm despite our snow-soaked clothes. The fireplace was switched on as my mom started making hot chocolate, and we all piled onto the couch. We snuggled up under too many blankets (though can you really have too many blankets?) as I flipped through the channels looking for something for us to watch. It seemed as though there was nothing but Christmas movies on; it was that time of year, after all. Eventually, we settled on Home Alone right as it was starting. How was I meant to get through the holiday season without watching it? Evangeline would have most likely killed me if I hadn't. Ever since we were little, it was the one movie we had to watch every single year. Though I would always complain about there being no Chanukah movies, Evangeline reveled in the Christmas spirit. I wouldn't say that she wished she wasn't Jewish, but her love for the holiday season went far beyond Chanukkah and Christmas. Winter was always her favorite season. While most people would be complaining about the cold and having to stay inside, longing for warm spring days and time spent out in the sun, she would always find a way to make the most of the smallest and hardest things she had to deal with.

Perri and I couldn't help but cuddle up on the couch together. I wouldn't say I didn't want to cuddle with her on the couch, but in front of all our friends felt like a huge step. This isn't me saying I'm not ready for that. I've been dying to tell them, but after spending so long not being able to tell them, or really just trying not to tell them, this public display of affection just felt like all sorts of wrong. But there was nothing wrong with us wanting to have a moment of public affection without our friends noticing and then putting it all together. Not that I have a problem with telling anyone that we're together. That's really just up to Perri at this point, but I guess there was some part of me that wanted to tell our friends. I wanted them to see us happy together and wanted them to see that they wouldn't have to worry about me.

Ever since Evangeline died, Kyle and Taylor have been acting like they need to protect me, like I'm fragile. Sure, I haven't been doing the best, but my sister died. That should have been expected, even if her death was unexpected. But since her death, everyone has been treating me like some fragile little porcelain doll that will break if you look at it the wrong way. I'm sure it would be really good for them to see me happy and doing well. I can't even begin to imagine the amount of pressure they must be feeling when it comes to just making sure that I'm okay. That's how Perri and I ended up together in the first place.

"You two look awfully comfortable, anything you're not telling us?" Kyle said as he made his way into the living room with a bowl of popcorn. Of course, he was hungry; that boy is always hungry.

"Got a problem with it, Ginger?" Perri retorted before I even had a moment to fully come to terms with what was happening.

"I haven't heard that since we were kids, Peregrine," Kyle said with a laugh.

I looked between both Kyle and Perri, shock written all over my face. "Peregrine? Your full name is Peregrine? How did I not know this?"

"I don't really like to tell people about that. I don't think any of my friends at school know." She laughed and then turned back to the movie without a second thought.

That wasn't good enough for Kyle, though, as he moved to stand right in front of the TV screen, blocking it from view. "Still didn't answer my question."

"What? We can't cuddle without it being something?"

"I never said that, but the two of you didn't even know each other before this week and now you're all cozied up on the couch. Don't make me the bad guy for being curious." With the look Kyle shot Perri, I knew we weren't going to win this. Sooner or later, we were going to be spilling everything out to him and, subsequently, Taylor. Not that I minded, of course, they were my best friends and it had felt odd not having them even slightly involved in one of the most important things to have happened in my life recently. They deserved to know.

"You're the one who stuck the two of us together for the whole trip, what did you expect? You didn't want to take care of me or be stuck worrying about me all week. She stepped up and actually seems to care. It was bound to happen. At least someone here really does care about me." I snapped, and honestly, I didn't mean to. I was just so fed up with the way everyone had been treating me. And the way Kyle felt as if he could just walk in and be a part of something that was so seemingly not his business just because I was me, without even seeing the way everything has changed in the past few months.

Kyle looked hurt. His face began to scrunch up, but as quickly as it did, he relaxed his features as to not let on to his pain. It was so typical of him to want to hide how he was feeling that I almost didn't register the hurt in his eyes. I had gone too far. I always did.

Perri put her hand on my shoulder. Even she knew I had gone too far with Kyle. We're used to pushing each other around like siblings, sure, but there's the jokingly way we normally push each other around, and then there's whatever I just pulled.

"Okay, Kyle, since you just had to be so nosy about it, we are dating, and if you have a problem with it, I believe you can find the door just fine, or do you need me to show you?" Perri was trying to bring back the banter from just moments earlier, though it was to no avail.

"I've got no problem with it, it's actually nice!" Kyle smiled, and I did feel the warmth from it as he spoke, "but I do think someone has some unresolved feelings about our little situation here."

"It was then my turn to laugh. Unresolved feelings were one way to put it. I don't think I've been subtle at all when it comes to how I'm feeling about any of this. "I guess I'm sorry if I gave off the impression that I was ever completely okay with any of this. My sister died and then you used Perri as a way to not have to deal with my problems for a week. I get it, you don't want to deal with my shit, and honestly, you shouldn't have to. But everyone keeps acting like I'm this fragile little doll and I'm not. My little sister died, but no one has to treat me any different. And I know she was your friend too, I'm not trying to discredit that at all, but she isn't here this year to take me off your hands so here we are. You went ahead and found someone else. And I like her, I really do, and there is no one else I would have wanted to spend this week with, but I just can't figure out where you stand. Either you want to be my friend or you don't want to deal with me at all, just make up your mind."

Kyle looked even more hurt. Tears sprang to his eyes, and

he was doing all that he could to not start crying. "Aubrey, you've been my best friend for more of my life than you haven't been. Nothing is changing how much I love you. And I know you're hurting, and you know we all are too, and there is no version of my life where I wouldn't be friends with you. I didn't put you and Perri together because I didn't want to deal with you or your anxiety, I did it because— "

"Because I'm transferring to your school and I was nervous about making friends. That's what the phone call with my mom was about the other day." Perri spoke up, tears threatening to spill from those beautiful green eyes. "Our parents were really close growing up, and with the divorce and everything, me and my mom are moving in with Kyle and his family. At least for now. And I'll be living with my mom full time, so that's why I'm here, that's why I was at the party, that's why all of this is happening."

I couldn't help but feel the smallest bit of excitement bubble up inside me. There was no reason our relationship was going to end when we all got back home.

"I'm sorry we all lied to you, but I'm not sorry that it brought me to you. And I know what I'm about to say is going to hurt you, and I'm so sorry, but a relationship built on lies is not a relationship that I want to be in. I wish it didn't have to come to this. If we can figure this out without all the lies, maybe then we can actually work this out, but neither one of us should want something that we built on this mountain of lies and misunderstandings. I'm sorry."

Perri got up and left before I could get a word in. Of course, I had blown everything up. The movie was still playing, but none of us were paying attention in the slightest. It was the only thing keeping me from just falling apart right there in the middle of the living room. I had ruined everything.

❄

By the time the movie was over, our parents were all filing back into the room, spirits high, ready to light the candles for the sixth night of Chanukah. At this point, there weren't many gifts left to give out, if any, so it was nothing more than the symbolic lighting of the menorah and reciting of the same prayers as always. It was weird this year without Evangeline. Normally, by the sixth night, she would be going on and on about how lucky we all are to spend time together as there was always someone (usually Kyle or Taylor's brothers) who would be complaining about not getting any gifts. Evangeline would always remind us of how lucky we were to have each other, to have a roof over our heads, and to be on this wonderful vacation. But nothing about this night felt wonderful. Perri was refusing to leave her room. I couldn't blame her; I had been seriously awful to everyone in that room. I didn't know who I was becoming, but I didn't like it one bit. I didn't like the idea of not having Perri by my side. We could find a way to navigate our new relationship despite the small lies it was built upon. Sure, we were both in the wrong, but she had been the one person that was able to get me through almost anything on this mountain, and now she just wanted to walk out of my life as if none of it had existed?

She could never walk out of my life, though. Not only had she become such a major part of it, but she was now moving in with my best friend. No matter what she wanted to try, she wasn't going to be getting away from me anytime soon. I just needed to figure out the right thing to get her back.

Chapter Twenty

I had stormed off to my room to cool down. I hadn't meant to explode. Perri hadn't meant to explode, at least I hope she didn't. I so badly want to point the blame anywhere else, anyone else, but I know that it needs to fall onto my lap. I did this to myself. Everyone was just trying to be nice to me, and the guilt I've been feeling this whole trip just took over. I've spent this whole trip drowning. It's almost as though I'm stuck in a frozen lake, just under the surface, unable to break through. But when I thought there was no way out, when I was all but ready to drown, Perri showed up and smashed through the ice and pulled me back to safety. She pulled me out of the freezing water and helped me finally feel okay again. Even if it was just for a moment. Yet all I could do was push her away. I didn't even think for a second about what she might have been going through. Her presence on this trip was in and of itself filled with so much pain, and I just ignored that in favor of my own shit. She needed me just as much as I needed her, and I wasn't there. She had been able to put all of her shit aside for me, and I couldn't seem to give her the same grace in return. How shitty does that make me?

I sat on my bed and finally let the tears fall. Once they started, there was no way of getting them to stop. Everything was finally bubbling over and I finally let myself feel all the hurt I had been trying to ignore since we landed here in Park City.

There was a soft knock on my bedroom door, and then the door creaked open. I looked up for a minute to see Taylor standing in the doorway. She seemed hesitant, almost scared, and shit, that was all my fault.

When I didn't say anything, Taylor slowly made her way across the room and sat on my bed next to me. I looked up at her and, without even having to say a word, she pulled me into a big hug. We sat there like that for a moment. Just the two of us.

I don't know how long Taylor held me for, but in that moment, we said everything that we had been so scared to say for the last little while. Her love for me and the way she cared for me spoke louder than words in that moment. With her by my side, I felt as if everything was going to be okay again. Maybe this was because our relationship has always seemed rocky. I guess we've always fought like sisters. I've known her my whole life; we've been so close for so long that she always seemed like another sister to me. She was just as much a part of our family as Evangeline or I was.

I also couldn't help but be jealous of her, especially when we were younger. She was everything I wasn't. She was tall and skinny, and everyone loved her. She was afraid of nothing. Anyone in their right mind would have wanted to be her. I always wanted to be her. I grew up living in the shadow of my best friend. I'd never be anywhere near as amazing as she was. I could only dream to be. She could be friends with anyone she wanted. Everyone wanted to be her friend. She was always so cool; it just made sense. Yet, for some reason, she refused to leave my side. She was never friends with the popular girls because that meant leaving me behind. They never wanted to be friends with me. They never had any desire to be in the same room as me outside of class. That was all I wanted. Someone to notice me and see me for who I was.

Then Kyle came along, and somehow he wanted to be friends with me just for me. At first, I don't think he even wanted to be friends with Taylor, if that was possible. He refused to spend any time with me if she was around. I thought that was the weirdest thing; everyone else wanted to be around her, why didn't he? I think I decided he just had a crush on her. To little middle school me, that was the only thing that seemed to make any sense. Who knew Kyle would be way too gay for both of us. He would never even imagine dating one of us. That might be my favorite thing about him. But when we were in middle school trying to fit in, the last thing he was sharing with us was the fact that he liked boys.

Taylor and I sat on the bed in silence for about half an hour before either one of us dared to speak. It felt wrong without Kyle right next to us. I had been so used to it always being the three of us that his absence was quite heavy. But he needed to be with Perri. Of course, he had to. I didn't fault him for being with her instead of me; she was his cousin after all, but it still hurt that he wasn't sitting on my other side, wrapping me in a large hug, comforting me as I felt my world was ending.

"We don't have to talk until you're ready, but if you're ready, I'm here." For the first time in what felt like forever, I finally stopped crying. "I'm going to be really honest with you. I might not be saying what you want to hear, but I do think this is what you're going to need to hear."

I sighed and rested my head on her shoulder. "I know I messed it all up, if that's what you're going to say. I'm a self-centered bitch who can't seem to see past her own problems. You can pass up on that lecture."

She looked at me and then burst out laughing. If I wasn't

in such a crappy mood, I might have started laughing along with her. "Is that really what you thought I was going to say? What kind of a friend would I be if I wasn't immediately on your side? Now that's not to say what you did isn't shitty, it is. But what she did was just as shitty. You both overreacted."

"I didn't want that to happen. I didn't want to split us up over this. I just hate being babied. Ever since Evangeline died, I've been babied by everyone. I just want to be treated like a normal human being."

"I know, and I don't know what I could say to make this any better."

"I'm just so mad that I let everything get in the way of this relationship. Like I've been falling head over heels for her and now it's all gone to waste. I don't even care about those little lies. She was doing what she needed to protect herself. I understand that more than anyone. But I drove her away. How am I supposed to fix that?"

"There's still time. The trip's not over. You still have time. You can fix this. Kyle and I are here to help. You've got two days left to fix this and we're all on your side. We're all here to help."

Chapter Twenty-One

When I woke up, the realization hit that we only had today and tomorrow left of the trip. I wasn't ready for the trip to be over. I just don't want to have to be pulled back down to reality where things have to get all complicated. Just going back to normal life is complicated as hell. I mean, I'm not scared to go back to school; it's just going to be so different. I don't know if I'm fully ready to brave coming out at school. I love everything Perri and I have been doing, and I don't want to just throw that away, but some of the people at school can just be so mean. It was already so hard for Perri to be comfortable with telling Taylor and Kyle, so school is a whole other monster, and if I don't fix this mess, it's only going to get worse.

I know that's not something I should really be worrying about, after all, we're graduating soon anyway. Whatever happens when we get back to school shouldn't be such a big deal. I just don't want to disappoint my community and the community that I have grown up in. I have been at this school all my life and while I would hope everyone would still love me just as they have since I was little, I know that just won't be the case.

I got out of bed and got dressed with all these worries floating around my head. The other thing I would need to do would be to come out to my parents. That's a monster I don't know if I'll ever be ready to face, but I might not have a choice.

I didn't want to be worrying about this. It's not like it's something I can control; in fact, it's the exact opposite. I guess that's why I'm stressing about it, but I really don't want to be stressing so much. I guess the only way to stop stressing would be to talk to Perri. In some way, we established that we do like what we're doing right now, but the future is so unknown that even what we talked about days ago could have completely changed.

I ate breakfast quickly, trying to avoid talking to my parents as much as possible. I got ready to ski just as I would on any other day. I played music a bit louder than I usually would to try and distract myself from the buzzing going on in my head. Doing my skincare and makeup did help me a little bit to take my mind off my crazy brain and the craziness that was going on up there.

I didn't want to have to face the topic of the future with Perri. I was totally scared of what she would say. I mean, I don't think she would be evil or anything. We both told our parents about each other; it's not like she's planning on breaking up with me here and now on this trip, but it's not like that's not a possibility. The idea is still out there. Perri could decide tomorrow that she doesn't want to do this when we get back to school, and although that might tear me apart, I would just have to accept it and move on from this.

This morning, Perri didn't welcome me as she did every morning. We got on the bubble and started to make our way to the top of the mountain to begin skiing for the day without a word. I was incredibly anxious the whole time. We were both hurt and in turn, hurting each other, but I couldn't help but feel like it might as well be for the better. I had been making everything worse and everything about me anyway. I just had to push the thoughts away so that I would just deal with it later.

Kyle and Taylor got off the bubble at the first stop. I don't think I've ever gotten off at the first stop and honestly wasn't planning on trying it any time soon. Then it was just the two of us.

"Perri, can we please talk about last night?" I asked in some attempt to try and patch things up.

"What's there to talk about?"

"Come on, we've been having such a great time this week, we're not going to throw that away, are we?"

She didn't get a chance to answer as the lift came up to its final destination and we had to get off. We went straight to Saddleback from the run without questioning it. Today was going to be a chill day. I mean, she wasn't okay, and I was anxious, so we just needed to take the day to be chill and just get back into being ourselves.

The silence between us on the lift was a heavy silence, full of all the things we didn't know how to say. There was so much we needed to say to one another, and it was evident in the way we were sitting on the chair. I wanted to ask, but I feared that maybe I would be overstepping. I know she always worries about overstepping or saying too much or asking too much or whatever, and now I knew how she felt when she would try and talk to me and try to make things better when it came to my sister. I just wondered what could be going on. What could be wrong.

The first few runs of the day were almost awkward as we found our rhythm in silence. I knew that I would have to wait until lunch to talk to her, and the pressure that I was putting on myself was eating away at me. I didn't want to wait until lunch to talk to her. And sure, it looked like there would be plenty of moments where I could have spoken with her, but every time we got on a lift, there was always another person or two on the lift with us, and I couldn't imagine having to talk to her about something so deep while others could listen in. This was a moment for the two of us to be together and really talk through everything.

I screwed up. I know that. I hadn't even thought for a second about how any of this might impact Perri. That was just so stupid. Of course, it would impact her. I've been practically dumping my shit on her all week, and she hasn't even made a fuss, even when she's been going through some really tough shit herself. I didn't even think about her. I knew from the start she was going through a really tough time, no matter how much she put a smile on her face and acted as if everything was okay. It wasn't.

I needed to do something big to make it up to her. Something huge. But I was out of ideas. Anything I could possibly think of wasn't good enough. I was going to need backup.

When we made it to lunch, still not talking, I shot Kyle a quick text. He would be the best person to help me with this.

After we went in for the end of the day, I immediately went to find Kyle. Luckily, he wasn't too busy and was almost ready to head into town with me. I knew it was a lot to ask for him to come into town with me on such short notice, but if we were going to be quick on our toes, we were going to make this work.

But was talking to Kyle really what I should have been doing? If this were to go badly, I could easily lose Kyle, not that I think I would lose him. I don't think that would happen in a million years, but if it had to come down to it, I don't doubt for a second that he would choose his cousin over me. That's obvious. Of course, family would come first. So then, Kyle would want to help me, right? He would want to come into town with me and spend time trying to figure out the perfect way to make it up to Perri. If anything, he should have a handful of ideas of things she would like.

Kyle should be the best person to go to with this. Maybe I

should invite Taylor too, have the three of us go and figure this out together. Whatever I end up getting for Perri has to be perfect. I'm not just trying to save my relationship with her, but it almost feels as though I'm trying to save my entire friend group. The last thing I want to do is put Kyle in a position where he would feel like he has to choose between Perri and me. I'm going to make this right.

I found Kyle in the lobby, already waiting for the shuttle to take us into town. I took a deep breath, smiled, and walked over to him. Things would only be awkward if one of us made it awkward, and I wasn't going to be the person who made it awkward today.

When I approached him, he just looked scared. I guess I couldn't blame him. I'd be scared in his situation too. He had almost successfully set up his cousin and best friend, and the second he found out about it, it all went to shit right in front of his eyes. I was scared too. Was I about to lose my best friend? Was this going to be the last time I really got to enjoy spending time with Kyle before it all went to shit? It couldn't be. I couldn't let it be.

Before Kyle or I got a chance to say anything, the shuttle pulled up and we were on our way into town. I reached into my pockets, searching for my headphones so that I could just listen to music and tune everything out during the short ride to the top of Main Street. Silently cursing at myself, I realized I must've left them in the condo. Of course, I did. But right when I started to worry about how I would either start a conversation with Kyle or just stare out the window and deal with the quiet of the empty shuttle.

Then Kyle's hand bumped mine, and he held out an earbud with the goofiest grin on his face. A peace offering (if one was even needed), and I took it with a smile as he draped his arm around my shoulders. I didn't mean to curl into him, but we've grown up so close like this that it was just what I did before I could even realize it. And then we were at the top of Main Street, climbing out of the shuttle and back into the frigid air of winter.

"So, what's our game plan, chickadee?" Kyle asked as we began walking down Main Street.

"I don't really have much of a plan. I have no idea what I want to get her. I just know it has to be perfect. She has to want to take me back. I need to make things right between us. I'll get whatever will do that. I'll get anything for her."

"That's so not helpful. We don't have enough time to be going into every single shop on Main Street hoping to find something. That's not going to work, and you know it. We need some sort of a plan. We need something. Are we thinking jewelry, food, something else?" I shot him a look that seemed to convey how absolutely lost I felt in that moment. "You have absolutely no idea, do you?" He sighed and started to laugh, "We're going to have to go into every single one of these stores to try and find the perfect thing for her, aren't we?"

All I could do was look up at him and smile my most innocent smile. He shook his head and draped his arm around my shoulders, and we started walking down Main Street.

Chapter Twenty-Two

We must have walked into about twenty different shops. Nothing seemed to have anything close to what I would have wanted, though to be fair, I probably wouldn't have known what I wanted if it slapped me across the face. All I knew was that it had to be perfect. But how was I supposed to even know what was perfect? I wanted whatever I would buy for Perri to be something that was cute, but also something that would be meaningful. But not too meaningful, or expensive. But not cheap. It had to make some sort of an impact. How was I going to find one thing that was going to encompass everything I wanted to say to her, and the wonderful experiences we had on this amazing trip together at the same time? Was there even a gift that was going to be able to do it all?

Kyle and I walked into the last store, and all I could do was hope and pray that I would find the perfect gift sitting right there in the store. Whatever I was looking for had to be there. I searched each and every aisle of the store, hoping for the one thing that I knew would be perfect. Then I saw it all the way in the very back of the store. Most people wouldn't have noticed it. I doubt it was even put there by someone who worked at the store, but it was everything I needed it to be. It was a pamphlet, most likely left by a previous tourist who had been distracted by one of the beautiful items in the store. A dog sledding advertisement, with a coupon code and everything. All I could do was hope that they weren't booked for the day. An afternoon of dog sledding would be the perfect thing for Perri. She'd absolutely love it. And the offices that were advertised in the pamphlet were just down the street. The walk wouldn't be long at all. We'd definitely be able to make it over there, make our reservation, and then get back in time for candle lighting and presents. The pamphlet would be the perfect thing to wrap for her too.

I practically ran into Kyle when running to find him. The smile he shot me told me he knew exactly what I was trying to say. He looked at the pamphlet and address and just nodded. It was going to be perfect, and we were on our way.

"Just make sure your group is ready and in your hotel lobby at one p.m. sharp for my guys to come pick y'all up. The drive is about an hour, but you'll be in for a load of fun when you get there." The woman at the storefront couldn't have been more helpful. "And don't forget to show my guys these tickets so they know I sent you. They always treat my guests exceptionally well." She winked at Kyle and me, probably assuming we were a couple and the tickets were meant to be some form of a double date, and then we were off to call the hotel to make sure we got a van back just in time. Everything was finally falling into place.

When we got back to the hotel, I immediately took a quick shower. I wasn't willing to be gross from skiing when giving Perri this gift. I wanted to make a large impact with the gift and the experience, and being somewhat smelly from skiing was not how I wanted to be handing over this gift. It deserved the right amount of love and care put into every second of it. Perri deserved someone who would give her their best as often as they could, and I needed to be that for her, especially tonight. She deserves someone who doesn't let their own shit get in the way of the relationship, and I'm done putting my mess before our relationship. I am here and going to be present in every way that I can. It's the least I can do for her. Showering is simply the bare minimum. It's the least I could do.

We'd be having dinner before gifts, as usual, and I was determined to make the whole thing special. The restaurant that we were going to wasn't one of the super fancy ones, but I was going to dress up just a little bit. Just enough to make it special. I was determined to make this night absolutely perfect in every way.

I was almost late to meet up with everyone for dinner. I had to make sure my makeup and outfit were just right. I thought about skipping blow-drying my hair to save on time, but going outside in Utah in the middle of winter with wet hair doesn't sound like a good idea. I was wearing my navy sweater dress that I only bring out around this time of year, paired with a pair of tall black boots. I always pack this outfit just in case the need arises. I've packed it for three years now without actually wearing it.

Luckily, the restaurant we were going to was in one of the hotels and just across Canyons Village. It was one of the nicer restaurants, and with a group as large as ours, we had rented a private room so that we could all dine together without having to be split up into two or three separate tables. Also, with it being the sixth night of Chanukah, and the second-to-last night of the trip, we tended to go all out. We always let the last night be super chill because we would put a lot of focus on packing our suitcases after a full day of skiing and the craziness that can be returning our rentals, so we decided that the second-to-last night of the trip was the one we would make super special.

The walk was short. The hardest part was wrangling Taylor's brothers and trying to keep them close by while we tried to make our way over to the restaurant. Luckily, I wasn't stuck on babysitting duty that night (or ever) because those kids were really a lot to handle. I don't know how anyone does anything with them around.

I was walking sort of next to Perri, and by that, I mean I was walking next to her but not intentionally, and we weren't talking even though I wanted nothing more than to hear her laugh at something stupid I would have said. It was probably for the best; I was buzzing with nerves and sure I was going to say something stupid and make a total fool out of myself if I even dared to open my mouth. Kyle and Taylor were whispering a few paces ahead of us, no doubt talking about my master plan for tomorrow (well, tonight and tomorrow, I guess), and I couldn't help but worry it would all go to shit.

I wanted to talk to Perri, of course I did, but there was a part of me that felt the second that I would open my mouth, it would all devolve into chaos and I would lose her forever.

Luckily, we made it to the restaurant faster than I had expected. I couldn't wait to sit down and get dinner over with. This meal that had always been one of my favorites was now one that I couldn't wait to get through so that I could get to the rest of the night.

Of course, the dinner was long. It had to be, right? I wanted nothing more than for the dinner to pass so we could get to Chanukah, and dinner seemed to drag on forever. It felt as if it was an hour before the appetizers were served, and this big celebratory meal wasn't one where we would be skipping dessert.

I spent all of dinner sitting next to Perri. I wish I could say we talked and got back to our normal rhythm with nothing to worry about, but that would be a lie. She barely even looked at me when I asked her what she was planning on ordering. And Kyle was trying so hard to get us talking to each other, and while I was willing to give some longer answers, Perri's responses to anything Kyle was saying were short and clipped. She barely gave him anything to work with. Maybe tonight wasn't going to work out in the way I had hoped. Perri seemed to be mad at the world, and how was I supposed to do anything to change that?

When dinner was finally over, I couldn't have been more relieved. I would have done just about anything to have gotten out of that restaurant. Throughout dinner, my heart was racing, and I felt as if my throat was closing no matter how much water I drank to try to loosen it. I could barely eat my food, and with it being one of the nicest meals we were going to have during the trip, I couldn't help but feel bad about the whole thing. My parents were spending a lot of money on this meal, and I was barely able to eat anything from the prefixed menu that was put in front of me. Though the only person who really seemed to notice was Kyle. Every single time he would look over at me, concern would flash over his features. The food being put in front of all of us was delicious and the kind of food that everyone at the table would have been expecting me to devour, yet just looking at my plate made me feel as though I was going to throw up.

When we walked through the door into the condo, I couldn't even start to relax. I wanted to. I wanted to believe that the night was going to go as planned and things would be okay between Perri and me after this, but it felt like such a big ask out of the situation. I had really been awful, hadn't I? There was no reason she shouldn't forgive me for screwing it all up. It would just make sense if she didn't. I could be okay with that. I'd have to be. I'd have to make peace with the fact that all of the wonderful things that happened this weekend were for nothing. They'd just have to be a good memory and nothing more. It would be what it had to be. I'd deal with it. I'd move on.

Everyone gathered around the counter where the menorah sat. I had the envelope with Perri's gift in my hands and couldn't keep them from shaking. I tried to will them to remain still, but I wasn't having much luck with that. The matches were lit, and as one of the parents lit the shamash, everyone began to sing the prayers. I joined in because what else was I supposed to do? I sang softly, and for the first time during the whole trip, my focus had been turned from the loss of my sister to something that finally felt more important. Not to say her death and my grief weren't important. But I couldn't just sit in it forever. Though I wouldn't say moving on would be the answer, I could at least allow myself to enjoy the life I've been given, even if she isn't here. She wouldn't want me to be suffering with such crippling grief as a result of her death.

Perri came over to me before I could even make it over to her. It was almost as if she teleported from across the room the second the prayers were done. She had a small gift bag in her hands and what I could only hope was the same scared look I had on my face.

She looked down at her feet as she began to speak to me. "I lashed out at you yesterday and you didn't deserve that. You definitely didn't deserve to get broken up with over that. I seriously overreacted."

"Perri, you didn't. If anyone fucked up it was me." I interrupted her. I had messed up. If anyone was at fault, it was me. She shouldn't be taking the blame.

"Please just let me finish," she said with a sigh as she looked up at me. "I just want to make things right. I know there's nothing I can say or do that will take back everything I said. It was so incredibly selfish of me to center myself in a situation where you were so clearly hurting. And as you know, things between my parents have been rather rough, and well, a lot of that had to do with lying to each other. I know that doesn't justify any of what I said, or any of the lies, but I hope it helps you understand. It might be stupid, but I wanted to get you a little something to say I'm sorry." She handed me the gift bag, and I almost started to cry then and there. But then I remembered the envelope in my own hands and knew what I had to do.

"No, it was selfish of me to center this entire trip and group in my trauma and my issues. You're going through your own stuff and it was selfish of me to ignore that. How are we supposed to be in this together if we can't see past each other's issues? And I don't care about the lies. They weren't anything too big, and you were doing what you needed to in order to protect yourself and your mental health. Anyway, I wanted to find the perfect thing to make it up to you. I hope this does it justice." I passed her the envelope and looked at her with pleading eyes.

"Only if you open yours first," she said with a cheeky grin spread across her face. It made me feel as though I was truly in the right place at that moment. I reached into the bag and pulled out a beautifully wrapped jewelry box. I carefully peeled off the tape and unfolded the wrapping paper to reveal the sleek black box. Perri was bouncing on her heels, anxiously waiting for me to actually get to her gift. It was quite a thrilling feeling, as though I was holding onto all of the power in that moment. But I wanted her to be able to get to my gift, and for her to be able to do that, I would have to actually open hers first.

I gently lifted the lid off the box, and sitting in the sleek box was a glittering charm bracelet. The bracelet had three charms on it that were evenly spaced out. The first charm was a glittering blue and silver snowflake. I gingerly ran my fingers over the charm before turning to the next one, which was a pair of skis. I ran my fingers over the skis, and my eyes started to well up with tears. Of course, Perri had thought to focus the bracelet on the trip we were on. The last charm surprised me. It seemed so different from the other two charms, but I couldn't help but feel like it fit so perfectly: a small silver key. It couldn't have been bigger than my pinky nail, but I ran my fingers over it just the same.

"I love it," I said through tears as I looked up at Perri. She pulled up the sleeve of her sweater, revealing a matching bracelet with matching charms. The only difference on hers was where mine had a key, hers had a small lock. I couldn't help the tears which flowed so freely down my cheeks. I didn't even think about the fact that I was probably smudging the makeup I had worked so hard on earlier in the day. It no longer mattered to me. She was all that mattered. Perri was all that mattered.

"Well, I don't know if this will even come close to comparing to that," I said, looking down at my feet as I passed Perri the envelope with the two tickets for dog sledding. She carefully opened the envelope. I felt as though I needed to sit on my hands to keep them from shaking. What if she hated it? What if she didn't want to go? What if I actually majorly screwed up and was somehow ruining this relationship with this little gift?

But then I looked up, and when my eyes met hers, I knew I had gotten the right thing. She looked absolutely astonished. "How did you know dog sledding was on my bucket list?" She asked with the biggest smile on her face, and I finally felt as though I had done something right.

"Well, you may have said something about it at some point," I said with a sheepish smile. I couldn't actually remember if she had mentioned it before, but it seemed like something that would be perfect for her in the moment.

Without missing a beat, she grabbed onto the collar of my shirt and pulled me in for a kiss. "I think we can say all is forgiven." She whispered against my lips in between kisses. Our last day in this magical place would be just as magical as our first.

Chapter Twenty-Three

Waking up on the last day of the trip was a shock to my system. I wasn't ready for my last day in my favorite place in the world and didn't want to deal with that just yet. And yes, I know that I will probably be back here next December, but December just feels so far away.

I really learned a lot during this trip. It's so easy to get lost in the little things and in the things that can just bring me down, but there is so much more to life than just the little things. I could have spent this entire trip as a mess of a person who was unable to handle the fact that my little sister killed herself a year ago, but I was lucky enough to be able to move past that and am so glad that I did. This trip was so much more than a distraction from the anger and sadness that had been boiling up inside of me for the past year; it helped me to conquer and overcome it. I conquered more anxiety than I thought I was capable of during this trip alone.

There was an air of sadness in the room when I walked into the kitchen to make coffee and breakfast. This has been our home away from home since we were little, and sometimes, I think I've grown more here than I have anywhere else. My anxiety is, and has always been, so prevalent here, and getting to just address it has always helped me to better understand it.

Leaving tomorrow means going back to a place that feels like it's trying to choose which version of me it wants to see. It's a place that likes the real me until I'm an anxiety-ridden, panicking mess. Then, it wants me to fake a happy smile and be the person everyone thinks I am and wants me to be. Here with Perri, I get to be my most authentic self the entire time.

I was incredibly sluggish getting ready; it was almost as if I could just stop time from moving forward by just slowing down. I wish it were that easy. I didn't want to have to get on the really long flight out of here tomorrow. It just really didn't sound appealing. There was just so much more that could happen here. Maybe one day I'll get to live here. That might just solve my problem. I wouldn't have to worry about feeling out of place at home because this wonderful place would be my home. Though I don't think my parents would be too happy about that, I'd be over the moon.

The closest I've felt to my sister in the past year has been on this trip and in this place. That has to mean something. That can't mean nothing. I can't just ignore that.

Maybe one day I'll make a life here. Maybe that will be with Perri.

We headed out for the day with the sadness of an ending trip written all over our faces. Perri embraced me quickly when we all met up by the lift. As we stood in line, it began to set in that we were all going home tomorrow. I had known that it was happening, but I wasn't ready to deal with that just yet. I could handle school and whatever would come with that, but there is no way I can handle my parents and the move that is to come.

It was like none of us knew how to start a conversation on the lift as we made our way up. The end of the trip weighed heavily on all of our brains. We didn't want to have to talk about the sadness we were all feeling when it came to the end of the trip. We all wanted to be having fun and enjoying the day as much as we could. We all just wanted to live in the moment.

We got off the lift and skied down to the Red Pine base area, where we decided on a time for us to have an early lunch together and made sure that Kyle and Taylor were both on board with it. They would have to be; we had plans, and if they wanted to eat with us, they'd have to do it on our time. Kyle and Taylor headed toward the Short Cut lift, while Perri and I headed over to Saddleback. At this point, taking Saddleback at the beginning of our day seemed to have become part of our routine. We had just started every day on this lift and these runs.

Perri wanted to go down Hurricane Alley, which would mean having to go down Kokopelli. I was somewhat anxious about Kokopelli, mainly because I never know how I am going to feel on the run until I get on it, but also because I already wasn't in the mental state to deal with my own anxiety today. Kokopelli also gets really frustrating because I've been on it so many times yet I can randomly get anxious on it.

We started heading down the run, and I felt the anxiety and panic sinking in. I mentally cursed at myself as I inched my way onto the run. I kept trying to tell myself to stay calm and not panic, as if that really would do anything. It was the last day, and I wasn't in the mood to have a panic attack, especially on this run. There are so many runs that I can have a panic attack on and not feel super guilty about. Kokopelli just is not one of them.

As I eased myself onto the run, I cautiously started to ski. I was in a small area as I made my first few turns and got a feel for the run. It wasn't long before I was confidently turning down the run. I was so very proud of myself for being able to just push through in that very moment. I had wanted more than anything to be able to push through and make it down the slope without panicking, and I got wonderfully lucky. I was able to do it.

We pulled up to the entrance of Hurricane Alley, and I was honestly excited to head down the run. I couldn't wait to experience it. It had been one of my favorite runs during a trip a few years ago, but my confidence on it has dwindled since, and I could only wish to gain some of that confidence eventually. Maybe this trip has given me the confidence boost I needed. Maybe I have learned something wonderful about myself on this trip. Maybe, I've accomplished something so very wonderful today. This trip has already been so wonderful for my anxiety, and I've already learned so much; it wouldn't hurt if there was just a little bit more left for me to learn on this trip.

We made our way onto Hurricane Alley, and I hoped that I would just have a wonderful time on the run and maybe for once not totally freak myself out over a small bump or patch of ice. I truly felt like I was asking for a miracle, but I was just hoping that I could get something really wonderful for once. Maybe I'd find something special here and be able to have a wonderful and fulfilling experience that I have been longing for on this trip.

I made my first few nervous turns, following behind Perri in her tracks. I tried to also follow the hardest part of the run, applying what I had learned about skiing on similar runs over the past few years. I was very much in my head, thinking about every turn. But for the first time on this trip, being in my head was actually a good thing. I was able to just focus on each turn one at a time. One of the best things for me to do while skiing, as I have learned, is to just focus on making the turn right in front of me and not focusing on the run as a whole. To just focus on the run as a whole has always been too much for me when the runs are more difficult. All I have to do is make the turn right in front of me and then the next one until I'm at the bottom or end of a run.

All I had to do was make that turn, and then focus on the next one, and before I knew it, I was at the bottom of the run. That's what happened with Hurricane Alley. I focused on making one nice turn after another, and before I knew it, I popped out on the other side of the run. Skiing down the rest of the way was easy once I was out of Hurricane Alley.

Perri and I then decided to take Snow Dancer two times before skiing down for lunch. We'd do it once with Flying Salmon, and the other time would be with the wonderful steep part that we have both come to love. We would then use our momentum from that steep part to get down the flat part of Chicane.

We got on the lift, and I tried to figure out how to start a conversation. I wanted to talk to Perri. There was so much to say, yet I was weighed down by the trip ending, and it was all I could think of.

"Are you excited to leave tomorrow and go back home?" I asked. It was a stupid question, and I knew that, but how else was my awkward self supposed to start this conversation with Perri?

"Kind of," she replied. "I really miss my mom and am really excited to see her, but other than that, I'm sad to be leaving, I guess. What about you?"

"I'm not ready to go home. Like at all. I just don't want to deal with the mess that is my life back home. Like the stuff with my parents and all that. I mean, I know I really only have a week to deal with the move and everything before we're back at school, but that week just feels like such a long time to have to deal with that. I'm not sure I'm ready to face that. Being out here has just been pretty chill and nice and honestly, I'd just like to stay here."

"I get that. Life can be so crazy sometimes, and it's just easier to avoid it and not deal with it."

"Exactly. But I guess I'll have to deal with it eventually so I might as well face it now. Well, tomorrow. But this is also my favorite place on the planet and I always hate leaving. I'll probably move out here and live out here one day. It's my perfect environment. The town is so cute and could totally fuel my little writing heart."

"I totally get it. I'd love to travel for work though. I mean, as a photographer, it would just be so nice to be able to go wherever I can to take gorgeous pictures. Maybe I'd have a gallery here one day, but I can't see myself settling down anywhere. Settling down would probably mean a commercial photography job for bat mitzvahs and weddings. And no offense to people who can do that, but I need to be fueled creatively, and bat mitzvah photo shoots just don't cut it for me. I admire people who can do that though. I think I'd just get bored."

"No, I get that. I'd want to travel too. I've thought about being a travel writer for a bit, but I think I just really want to write fiction. But I'd love to travel and experience life so that I could find and have more material to write about. I mean, I'm not saying I can't write about things I've never experienced, but I think it's just easier to write what you know, and the more life and experience, the more there is to write about."

"Maybe one day after we both finish school, whether that's just college or beyond, we could travel together around the world for a couple months and do that whole life experience thing."

"Maybe we'd backpack through Europe or something. Or maybe birthright. I've always wanted to go to Israel. But we've got a lot of time to think about that."

"Oh definitely. And maybe we'll settle down here and adopt some kids and have a beautiful family together in like ten years."

"The future can be whatever we make of it."

"We'll just have to wait and see."

We got off the lift and made our way over to Snow Dancer for the first time of the day. It had been a while since we had been down Flying Salmon, and I was really excited to head down the run again. Although the beginning was incredibly frustrating to ski down—well, more like ski up—once I'm past that point, the run becomes so much fun, and I just want to fly down it and have a wonderful time. And if I'm lucky, I'm able to just forget about what's going on for a minute.

After taking Snow Dancer a second time, we headed down Chicane. We were definitely going to take the bypass, but the entire run was one that was just always enjoyable and as I've gotten more confident skiing on ice, the run has gotten easier and more enjoyable. It felt freeing to be able to make carving turns and ski down runs with a sense of confidence that I didn't know I had.

I saw Kyle and Taylor out of the corner of my eye when we pulled up to a ski rack to take our skis off. While seeing them and having lunch with them was great, it reminded me that today was our last day and we would be going home tomorrow. I wasn't ready to go home yet, but when trips come to an end, what choice do you have? It was time to go home and go back to a reality that I wasn't ready to enter.

Lunch was fun. It was nice to get to spend some more time with Taylor and Kyle. It was a little weird because I had become so used to lunch just being Perri and me, but it was still really fun. Plus, being with Kyle meant that the lunch conversation was the weirdest and most random thing ever. I don't even know what he was talking about, but there are times where he just talks at us about whatever the hell he wants to rather than fully engaging us in what he's talking about. He was talking about something so random that none of us were really interested in it. However, Perri seemed to be so fully engaged and involved that she was practically just learning about the dumb stuff he was talking about. I just sat there enjoying watching her engage.

It was so beautiful how she really became part of our friend group during this trip. At the beginning of the trip, it really felt like we were our group and she was just hanging with us for the trip, but now it feels like she's supposed to be hanging out with us. She's one of us now and I couldn't be happier. When we get back to campus, it will be so much fun to have her hanging out with us in the courtyard. Especially since it's getting nicer out and Kyle will be pulling out his guitar and playing for us more in the nice weather. I can't wait for her to experience that with us. I wonder how she's going to feel about his music. I can't wait until Kyle and his band finally put out an album for people to enjoy because his music deserves to be heard.

After lunch, Perri and I hopped on Tombstone and headed toward Red Pine Road. We were heading in for the day, and while that might've seemed sad, I was thrilled about where we were heading. After braving Kokopelli that morning, I was feeling unstoppable as we skied down Red Pine Road. The run was really fun if I was in the right headspace. I always loved it. Actually, that's a lie. I've hated the run when it gets icy, but sometimes it can be fun, like today. Especially once we get down to the base area. We skied right past the gondola and over to the Short Cut lift. Though this lift is always one of the worst—it's pretty steep and it comes up behind you so fast you will easily be knocked down if you're not careful—there's something pretty intimate about being on a two-person chair. Even though there were tons of people around, it felt nice knowing it was just the two of us on the chair. It was as if there was no one else on the mountain with us, at least for a moment.

The lift is pretty short, and before we knew it, we were getting off and making our way toward Boomer. I've always had a love-hate relationship with the run. Since we'd be coming in toward the middle of the run, it was actually the part of the run I tended to enjoy. But it's one of those runs where it always depends on the day and the conditions. I've seen that run in so many different conditions that I never know what to expect anymore. But when Perri jokingly yelled, "race you to the bottom," as she started to head down the run while I was trailing behind on the flat part, I knew I couldn't even think about the conditions of the run; I just needed to go. And that's what I did. I was so focused on getting down the run first that I didn't even have to think about anything else. With the open run in front of me and not another person in sight, I closed my eyes for a minute. I didn't want to forget anything. I wanted to remember how it felt to ski confidently down my favorite runs and ski with a passion that made all of my worries melt away.

Just to make it clear, I won. Don't listen to what Perri has to say about that race. I beat her fairly by a second. And just because her skis are longer, they got there first, but my body got to the bottom before hers did.

Chapter Twenty-Four

We were laughing as we made our way inside the hotel. Though it looked as though we were going to return our skis as we had done, this would be our last time. Luckily, our hotel made it super easy for us to return our skis, and all we had to do was say something to the person who was collecting our equipment, and they would take care of it for us. That was one less thing for us to have to worry about.

We quickly made our way back to our condos to drop off our helmets, goggles, and any other equipment that we needed to return to our rooms. I left my ski boots by the door as I had every other day of this trip. My parents would be taking care of that for me. I traded my ski boots for my after-ski winter boots and my helmet for the turquoise hat I had been refusing to wear throughout the trip. My braids were messy, but under the hat, they didn't look all that bad.

I was startled by a knock on the door, and I knew Perri was outside the door waiting for me. It was time to head down to the lobby and get ready to go.

We made our way down to the lobby with perfect timing. We had about ten minutes before anyone from the dog sledding company was going to be picking us up, giving us the perfect amount of time to grab a hot chocolate from the lobby before we were introduced to our guide. He ushered us out to the van, and within a few minutes, we were on our way to the mountain. There were a few other couples in the van with us; they seemed nice enough, but we kept to ourselves mostly. It was probably better that way. This moment was supposed to be about us after all.

The ride was about an hour long. When we arrived, the entire group was ushered out of the van into a small, shed-like building. We were then given the ground rules and were told about what was happening and what we would be doing.

During that, we were told that we would be going out in groups of four and we would be splitting up into pairs. Perri and I were, of course, going to be a pair, and the other pair we would be going out with was of course. There was no one else I wanted to experience this with. It didn't matter all that much to us who else we went with from the larger group that had scheduled for that day. As long as we were together, we were going to have the best time ever.

The groups of four were then asked to grab a time slot and pick when we wanted to go out in order of the groups. We got second. The first group went out and we were to wait. The first half of the groups that were going out were told to stay in the shed while the other groups went to play with the dogs. The shed was just so small that it was going to be hard for all of us to sit in there and wait. Plus, the cute dogs were going to be so fun to play with.

The first group left, and the bunch of us were all just sitting in the little room. It was nice and cozy and warm. Half of the people in here were either half asleep or fully asleep, while the other half was sitting, just mindlessly scrolling through their phones. There were a few people who were excitedly talking about what was going to be happening, but that was just a small bunch.

The two of us were just sitting there, somewhere in the middle. Perri was practically asleep on my shoulder (which was just really cute), while another couple was talking about the last time they went dog sledding. They were trying to include me in the conversation, but I wasn't really listening. I was too distracted by my girlfriend asleep on my shoulder to pay attention.

It wasn't very long until we were called to go out with the dogs. I was both excited and nervous as we walked outside. The group before us was just finishing up and told us that we were going to have a wonderful time before they went to go play with the dogs.

We then made our way over to the guides we would be working with. We started by helping them put harnesses on the dogs and getting them all set up. Another guide was walking the dogs that had just been with the last group over to the dog houses with all the other dogs that weren't working at the moment. The guides then began to get the four of us situated and ready to go.

We split off into our two groups, each with a single guide to learn what we were doing. One of us would be standing on the back of the sled with the guide while the other would be lying in the sled, wrapped up like a burrito. Perri and I quickly decided that I would be the one lying in the sled while she would stand on the back of the sled with the guide. I was honestly very happy with that decision.

The guide got me situated first since that would be the easiest for them. I sat in the sled with a few blankets on and underneath me so that I would be warm, as I would be practically lying on the snow. Once I was completely cocooned, the guide went to help Perri understand what she would be doing. They made sure we were all ready, and then we were off.

The dogs were running in front of us as we were pulled along around the trail that they had made on the mountain for dogsledding. The view was breathtaking. The views from the mountain skiing weren't even close to as pretty as the view we got with the dogs. Maybe it was just because the dogs' cute little butts were in the pictures I was able to take. I loved every moment of the sledding. It was so nice even though it was so cold outside, especially with all the wind. I just found it refreshing.

Before I knew it, the dogs were slowing to a stop back where we had started just minutes earlier. Both Perri and the guide helped me climb out of my cocoon. We then helped the guides get the dogs out of their harnesses and brought them over to the rest of the dogs.

All of the dogs were just so cute; I couldn't stop myself from running over to play with them. I was having so much fun, and the dogs were so cute; I didn't want to stop.

When I got a chance to look up at Perri, I realized she had her phone out and was taking pictures of me. She just had the biggest smile on her face. I shot her a jokingly shocked look, and she just burst out into laughter as she continued to take pictures of me.

"Any of those good?" I asked as I stood up and made my way over to her.

"Oh of course they are!" she replied. "You might not like some of them, but they are the cutest fucking pictures I have ever taken. You're just so fucking adorable I couldn't keep myself. I wish I had brought my camera with me. I mean it was smart that I didn't since it could have gotten broken, but imagine some of these pictures with that camera's quality."

"Am I really that cute? Are you sure you're just talking about the dogs? They make everything cuter. If you were playing with dogs, I'd probably think you were ten times cuter."

"Oh yeah? You really think I'm only cute with cute animals?" she said with a laugh.

"Oh, for sure. Cute animals make everything so much cuter. Especially these cuties." I gestured to the dogs.

"Yeah?"

"Yeah."

"So, you think these dogs are cuter than me?"

"Maybe."

"Maybe?" I looked at her cute, flirty smile and kissed her right there. I didn't care who saw. It didn't matter if everyone saw or if no one did. I didn't care.

"Why don't we head inside and get some hot chocolate, huh?" Perri whispered in my ear once we pulled apart. I nodded in response, and we walked back to the shed to get some hot chocolate.

On the ride back to the hotel, I fell asleep on Perri's shoulder, and honestly, I would have stayed there forever. There was nowhere else I would have rather been in that moment. This was something I could get used to. Losing my sister might have torn me apart, but I had found something better (though nothing and no one could truly be better than my sister). I had found love, and with everything else, that might've been the one thing that could've kept me going.

When we made it back to the hotel, it was time to start packing and get ready to leave bright and early the next morning. I couldn't believe the whole trip was over. In a matter of hours, we would be boarding a plane back home and leaving the magic of this trip behind. That was the last thing I could have wanted, truly. I wished we could just stay in this bubble forever.

My dad ordered pizza from one of the nearby restaurants and started blasting music as we began to pack everything. I grabbed my suitcase out of the closet we had left them in and went into my room. I didn't know where to start. There was the pile of mostly unread books on the nightstand, all of the clothes I had packed for the evenings, my bag of laundry, a handful of shoes, and whatever clothes I had that were still clean. This doesn't even scratch the surface though. There was also all of my ski clothes and gear, but all of my outer layers (not including my jacket which I would be wearing on the plane) were still somewhat damp, and it wasn't necessarily time to pack those just yet. I wanted them to dry at least a little bit more before I went into packing them. My helmet, gloves, and goggles were getting packed in the same place with my parents, and we normally take them in a carry-on because they are the more delicate items that we're packing.

Though packing was tedious, once I got into a groove with it, it was pretty easy. I left the last pocket of my large rolling duffel bag for my ski pants, fleeces, and any other big items. Though I still had my toiletries to pack in the morning, everything seemed to get packed quickly, and before I knew it, I was curled up on the couch waiting for my parents to finish packing all of their stuff. I grabbed the singular book I had left out for the long flight back home tomorrow and curled up on the couch with a plate full of the pizza my parents had ordered. The music faded into the background as I began to fall into the fictional world on my lap in front of me. I even forgot about the slice of pizza that was sitting on the plate to my left.

I don't think I even looked up until I felt the couch dip beside me. When I looked up from my book for the first time in what had probably been an hour, I was surprised to see Perri sitting next to me. She looked almost shy as she sat next to me, smiling. She had a plate with two slices of pizza, and I, almost instinctively, curled into her and got comfortable before turning back to my book.

Chapter Twenty-Five

I woke up early to finish packing and to get ready for the flight and day ahead of me. I packed up the rest of my toiletries and made sure my suitcase was closed and locked before heading into the living room, dragging it behind me. I was doing everything I could to keep myself awake at such an early hour and waited for my parents on the couch, fighting the fatigue that threatened to pull me under.

Before we were cleared by my father to actually leave the room and head down for checkout, we made sure to check every drawer and closet to ensure we weren't leaving anything behind before we left.

To me, this process of checking every space was my way of saying goodbye to the space. I know that might seem weird, but it has always provided a sense of closure for me on any given trip. We were all upset about leaving. I was especially upset, however. I mean, I always am. I really, truly feel that I belong here and that my life is here. I might go to college here, but eventually my life path will lead me here.

We sat in the lobby, waiting for the shuttle that would be coming to pick us up and take us to the airport, and I did my best to take in every last thing. I took in everything from how the lobby was decorated in the springtime to what the lobby smelled like in that moment. Kyle plopped down next to me. He put his arm around me as he realized what I was doing. He always tells me I have a certain look on my face when I'm trying to really take in every moment of something. He didn't say anything when he sat down next to me, though. I wanted to stay present for as long as I could, or at least just a little bit longer, and he could see that written all over my face. Once I would get on the plane, I would allow myself to slip into that anxiety, only to be able to push it away as I bury myself in a book or multiple books throughout the flight.

We sat in the lobby for another ten to fifteen minutes before the rest of the group was in the lobby, and then we were all ushered onto the bus. I comfortably sank into a window seat next to Perri. I wasn't entirely sure if she understood the mental gymnastics that I was going through in the moment, but I knew she was trying to. It's just so hard to leave the place that I have considered to be my real home and a place where I feel like I belong. And no matter how easy the transition back to normal life is, it can still take a toll on you.

The forty-five-minute-long ride was silent. The majority of people on the bus had fallen asleep; the rest of us were in our own sort of trance. Perri had been up late packing and didn't get much sleep, so she passed out on my shoulder as soon as she sat down next to me.

I spent the entire ride staring out the window. I always found the drive to and from the airport to be so beautiful, and I loved watching the snowcapped mountains roll by my window as we drove.

We arrived at the airport two hours before we were to board the flight. We got through security relatively quickly. Well, as quickly as you can with a group as large as ours. Getting through the line only took about fifteen minutes, but we had to wait for every person to get through and get all of our stuff on the other end. It took an additional twenty to twenty-five minutes for all of us to get through as a group. It probably wouldn't have taken so long if we had just decided to split up by family. Really, it was Taylor's brothers who seemed to take forever anyway, but that's what you get when you travel with a group, I guess. Things could be worse, and this travel day was pretty easy compared to some of the others I've had.

Once we got through security, we made our way through the airport and found our gate. We left most of the bags with the parents who volunteered to sit with everything while us kids went off and wandered around on our own.

Taylor, Kyle, Perri, and I all began to venture through the airport, looking for a Starbucks. We all needed both coffee and breakfast. We would grab coffee at Starbucks and then either get breakfast from there too, or we might go somewhere else to grab some breakfast. We looked around quickly and decided it would be best to grab food from Starbucks as well as coffee.

The line for Starbucks was long, but we had about an hour before boarding and we didn't have anything else to do besides get food and eat it before we boarded.

We were in line for a while. I was getting a bit antsy after about fifteen minutes because I just really wanted coffee, but I understood that there weren't many people working and it was probably one of the busiest times of day for them. I was also very hungry and really wanted one of their breakfast sandwiches.

Eventually, we got to the front of the line. Taylor went first, then Kyle, Perri, and finally, myself. Once we got our orders, we went back to the gate to sit and eat there. We all sat in silence as we ate. The airport around us was bustling with people traveling to new places and coming home.

I didn't want to go home. I didn't want to have to deal with the mess that would be my home. I didn't want to go back to a place that was a constant reminder of everything I've lost instead of this wonderful place that just reminded me of everything I've gained on this amazing trip.

After I finished eating, I took out my book and started to read. I honestly just wasn't in the mood to deal with people. I knew the day was going to be rough, as most travel days are, but my mind felt like it was on fire. Maybe coffee wasn't a good idea, but I didn't want to be falling asleep on the plane. I needed to save that for the minute I got home so that I could just pass out and not deal with my parents.

When I looked up from my book, Kyle was staring at me. He wasn't doing it in a creepy way; it was more concerned than creepy.

"Hey, do you want to go grab some snacks for the flight?" he asked, knowing that I can never say no to snacks.

"Sure," I replied, and we got up and went to go find a place that was selling snacks.

"You're not okay," he stated matter-of-factly when we got far enough away from Taylor, Perri, and the rest of the group.

"Yeah," I said in a whisper. I was going to cry. I felt it. Tears were beginning to well up in my eyes and I could feel them threatening to spill over. I didn't want to cry, but sometimes it feels like I just don't have a choice.

"Want to talk about it? We've got half an hour until we board and fifteen minutes until our parents want us to be at the gate, so while we're getting snacks you can just let it all out if you want. I'm here." I took a deep breath and, knowing that nothing I could say would change anything between Kyle and me, I began.

"Well, life's shit." Great start. "And I feel like I'm leaving the one place where I always feel like I belong and the one place that makes me feel like myself truly and fully. You know? It's just so fucking hard to get up and leave when I'm so fucking happy here. Also, I just don't want to go home. And you and I both know that the second I walk into that house, it is just going to be a disaster that I'm just thrust into the middle of my parents' shit, whether I like it or not. I know it might not be that long, but I just don't think I will be able to deal with that. Just not now, at least. Once school starts again, maybe I'll be able to get away, but until then, what am I going to do?"

"Hey, I get that. This shit's not easy. Any of it. But you know I'm not going anywhere. When you're home, I'm always a phone call or a text away, and you can always come knock on my door. That never changes. When we go off to college and shit gets bad and you just need someone who knows you like I do, I'm there. And I'm not going anywhere any time soon. Except to my house and then college hopefully, but you get what I mean." He got me laughing. What a wonderful thing it is to have a friend that can make you laugh when all you want to do is jump out of a window. I'm really lucky to have Kyle on my side.

We picked up some chips and other snacks and headed back to the gate. We were there five minutes before our parents wanted us to be, and it was perfect.

Before we knew it, we were boarding the plane to head home. The flight would be long, just like it had been on the way here, and I had a bunch of books that were eagerly waiting to be read. I was lucky to be seated in a window seat for the flight. I was supposed to be sitting next to Taylor, who would be in the middle, with Kyle sitting in the aisle, but Kyle might have said something to her because she switched seats with Perri and Perri sat between Kyle and me instead.

For the flight, I needed to zone out more than anything. I just needed a minute to myself. I took a minute and leaned my head on the window and did what I could to calm down before grabbing my first book and cracking it open to read.

After a while, the flight attendants came by with drinks

and the little free snacks. Other than that, I didn't look up from my book for the duration of the flight. The story kept me engaged and kept my thoughts focused on what was going on in the story rather than what was going on in my life.

I finished the book as the plane landed. I was home, and I really didn't want to be. But I still had a few hours before I would have to deal with my parents and the mess of the house I'd be going to.

We all disembarked from the plane and met with the group at the gate. Before we headed to the baggage claim, we stopped at the bathroom because, of course, at least one person in the group would have to go. We didn't wait too long at the bathroom; it was only fifteen minutes, tops. I didn't have to go, but at least half of the group did.

We then headed to the baggage claim, where we were to wait for the bags. It took another fifteen minutes for the bags to start coming down. We all waited by the baggage claim for our bags, and once we grabbed our bags, we stood off to the side to wait for the rest of the group.

We then left the airport and found our cars. For the first time since leaving for this trip, I was going to a place where my best friends weren't right next door, ready to annoy me or hang out or whatever. I don't think I could have been ready for going back home, though. Yet, I knew I would have to face it, and I wouldn't be facing it alone.

When I got home, the first place I went, surprisingly, was my sister's room. I walked in and didn't even turn the lights on. I closed the door behind me and just sat on the floor. I couldn't even bring myself to sit on her bed and mess with the last places she touched. But for the first time, I sat in that room surrounded by the person my sister used to be, and I didn't cry. At first, I sat there waiting for the tears to come. I could barely sit in that room without feeling the presence of what I could only assume was her ghost, and it would tear me apart every time. But this time, when I felt her sit on the floor next to me, I just smiled. She wouldn't have wanted me to wallow in the pain of everything she left behind. She'd want me to move forward with my life and be okay with it.

Epilogue

I didn't know who I was supposed to be on the one-year anniversary of my sister's death. I think everyone expected something different from me, and I couldn't blame them. I wanted to be the person who would be a total mess. Curl up in my bed all day and refuse to see anyone. I wanted to be the person who let this one day be used to wallow in the pain of losing my little sister, but I also knew I would never be that person. I'm not saying I'd moved on. I don't think losing your sister is something you can ever move on from, but I am saying that it's okay for me to keep that pain tucked away in a corner sometimes. I don't always need her by my side guiding me through every waking moment of my life. I'm allowed to be happy and to celebrate the great things that happen too. Just as I chose to celebrate my six-month anniversary with my girlfriend seeing my best friend, and her cousin, perform with his band for the first time.

I practically flew down the stairs when Perri knocked on my front door. This was going to be the date of a lifetime, and I couldn't have been more excited. I spent probably way too long making sure I looked the part. I didn't know if there was some sort of uniform that groupies are supposed to wear, but

I wanted to look cool. I wore my favorite dark skirt and flannel with exaggerated eyeliner and a dark lipstick to match. I felt cool. Perri looked hot in her cropped band tee and shorts. Six months strong, and I could barely keep my hands off her every time we were in the same room.

She grabbed me by the hand and walked me to her car, opening the passenger side door for me. I couldn't help but pull her into a kiss before we headed out to the show.

We met up with Taylor outside the venue so the three of us could walk in together. I was shaking with anticipation as Perri, Taylor, and I walked up to the concert venue. Kyle's band has been doing pretty well for the last few months, and he has been getting lots of gigs recently, but this was the first one I was able to convince my parents to let me come see. Perri had been to every single one of his gigs. I was envious of her, of course, but tonight was going to be special. Kyle had personally gone and begged my parents to let me attend the show. He said he wrote a song for me and I needed to hear it for the first time at the first show of the small summer tour he was going on. It was as close to a sendoff as we were giving him. At least that he'd allow.

The venue wasn't much more than a glorified bar, but as the three of us stood right in front of the stage, I couldn't have felt more at home. I looked around me and was so glad to be with my favorite people as we were about to watch my best friend go off on the coolest tour of his life. I couldn't have been prouder of him.

The room was beginning to fill up, and I stood there convinced every single person in that room was as excited as I was to be at that concert. I knew deep down a handful of them were only there because of the fact that it was practically a bar and a place most of the college students in our town liked to hang out at. I knew that's what Kyle's summer tour would mostly consist of, and he deserved so much better.

At least I would be content knowing the four of us would be going to college together in the fall. We got lucky with that.

The lights dimmed as the band walked on stage. Perri's arm wrapped around my waist as the drummer started playing. The room was vibrating as I heard each individual instrument come in, and the band started playing their first song. It was a cover of a popular song, one everyone in the room would know, and the energy in the room at that moment was unmatched. I wanted nothing more than to stay there forever. The lead singer's voice was beautiful, and it blended so well with Kyle's as he added some lower harmonies and background vocals. The whole thing felt so seamless. I felt lucky to even be a small part of the magic in the room that night.

The whole set flowed seamlessly. It was beautiful to watch. I loved getting to see my best friend in his element with my girlfriend by my side. It was everything I could have asked for and more.

Then there was a pause where Kyle went to the microphone to introduce the next song. It wasn't the first original song the band would be playing that night, but when he made eye contact with me, I knew it would be different.

"This next song I wrote about a year ago," he said into the microphone. He was doing everything he could to keep his voice from shaking and wavering, and I just wanted to hold him and make everything better. It should have been the least I could do in that moment. "I wrote it for a friend of mine and honestly, I never thought I would have the opportunity to get to play it for any audience, let alone her, but tonight I get to play it for her with a full band behind me and it is truly an honor. This song goes out to any and everyone who has dealt with loss of any kind. I see you; I feel you, and I promise you are not alone. This is Evangeline's Song."

Perri looked over at me with tears in her eyes, and that's when I realized the whole time she knew. She was in on it.

He started playing a really complicated riff on his guitar,

but when Kyle looked at me again, I could see the tears in his eyes. Hot tears ran down my cheeks as I listened to this song my best friend wrote after my sister died, and for the first time in over a year, I felt fully like myself again. I had chosen to surround myself with some of the greatest people in the world: my two best friends and my girlfriend. Even without my sister present, I knew she was looking after me and would help me get wherever it was that I would go next. I would make her, and the rest of the people I have chosen to surround myself with, very proud. I would make myself very proud. It was the least I deserved.

We spent the rest of the night singing and dancing and just having the time of our lives. I couldn't have been luckier to have had Perri by my side these last six months. Luckily, we'd be going to school together in the fall, but with Taylor moving away and Kyle leaving to go on tour with his band, Perri was going to be the one constant in my life, and I wouldn't have it any other way.

Acknowledgments

This book would not have been possible without the amazing people in my life who have guided me to this moment.

To my amazing parents for supporting my dreams and aspirations no matter how crazy they may have seemed.

To my brother Zach for always sticking by my side.

To my wonderful friends Nina, Madison, Kimberly, and Ellery for your continuous support of me and for being my sounding board at all times of the day or night.

To Falyn. You've seen this book every single step of the way. This story wouldn't be what it is without our many FaceTime calls at all hours of the day and night. Your unwavering support has meant more than you will ever know.

To my girlfriend Renea. Thank you for loving and supporting me through all the chaos.

To all of my lovely teachers. Your support has always had a deep impact on me.

To Nick, my kind editor for guiding me and shaping this book into something I am truly proud of.

And lastly, to every single person who has loved me and supported me through the many stages and phases of my life. To you all I am incredibly grateful.

About the Author

Jacqueline Elisabeth is a twenty-two-year-old author from New Jersey. She is currently a senior at Skidmore College majoring in Sociology with a double minor in English and Arts Administration. Her love for storytelling has led her to writing authentic stories about what falling in love looks like for queer and Jewish young adults.

https://jacqueline-elisabeth.wixsite.com/website